Luciano G

TUAREG HEART

ISBN

AUTHOR'S NOTE

It was not easy to portray the Tuareg people. The complex anthropology and numerous social layers of this population are disproportionate to its size. In the countries where they still live, Tuareg represent a small portion of the population. They number less than, for example, half a percent in Algeria. Precise and confirmed information is scarce. I had to acquire some rare books, watch documentaries in several languages, and carefully check every detail.

I described them as best I could. However, sometimes I needed to simplify so that the anthropological exposition did not overwhelm the story. I do not claim to have produced here a faithful presentation of this incredible people, surrounded by so many legends and myths. This is a book, primarily, of fiction. I use and abuse poetic license. I hope that those specialized in the subject, if any of them read this novel, will remember my freedom as a writer.

It has been a pleasure to dive into a world completely different from anything I have seen so far. I hope that you, the reader, find the same feeling as you embark on this adventure with me.

DEDICATION

Writing is what I would do every day, for free, without even needing a day off. It is that which makes me lose track of time, the space in which I can give voice to my truth. I dedicated countless hours of research for this book with love, attention, and the will to get it right. The difficulties, the hours when there was a lack of silence, the writing in the midst of the whirlwind of the daily life of a family with children. Not to mention that 2020 was a pandemic year, which added to all this the uncertainty about my work. But it is from difficulty, I believe, that creativity springs.

I dedicate this book to you, the reader, who has chosen to occupy your time reading my lines, from among so many other interesting things. A book without readers is the same as a song that nobody wants to hear. No art has value if it is hidden and does not allow other people to dialogue with the artist and debate their ideas. Art is made to build a bridge between the finite and the transcendent.

Reading transports people beyond the everyday and enables us all to touch the infinite. Whatever your spiritual beliefs, it is hard to accept that life is just work, bills, weekends. Sleep and then everything repeats itself. If it were that way, no one would appreciate a painting, a sculpture, a book. Nobody would cry hearing a foreign song, despite not understanding the lyrics, having been moved by its melody. Nobody would value love, friendships, the souls that touch us along the way. No one would seek nature to renew their strength. A bath in a waterfall, a walk in the woods. An incredible view of the horizon. The magic of the sunrise and sunset. Things that no matter how many times you do them, they remain incredible. There must be something transcendent. At least, that's the way I feel. That something is always waiting for us to cross that invisible bridge and believe—why not?—in the impossible.

THANKS

In a difficult time, publishing a book is more work than writing it. Believe it! Proofreading, editing, formatting, not to mention the cover, the design, and the printing. After all this, we still have to publicize it, and the author, sometimes introverted, doesn't know how and doesn't like to expose himself. I need to thank Mona Moraru, with whom I am working on this book to make sure the translation to English is as smooth as possible.

I must immensely thank my friend Leonardo Bandeira. After seeing the beautiful cover of his book *A Visão de um Pássaro* (A bird's-eye view) and following some of his work on Instagram, I knew I wanted him to be the mind behind my cover. Writer and designer (let him decide the order of these things!), he accepted my request without even knowing me personally. Together we founded Collective, through which I am launching this book. Leo and his family (Carol, Erick, and Ryan) give off an incredible light and energy! If you don't follow them on social networks, run there and do it right now. Beautiful images and messages through incredible photographs in the mountains of California, USA. To Leo, my many thanks!

Finally, I thank my family for the countless times when I was tired and irritated from going to sleep late and waking up early. All the effort directed towards finishing the book was done around the family's routine, in the hope of not disturbing them. Forgive me for almost always having one foot in reality and the other in fiction. Fábia, Júlia, and Sofia, I hope that one day you will read and treasure this work that I did with much dedication and love. I am in no hurry—I know that this day will come.

FOREWORD

It is a strong book. Well conducted. The plot offers several detailed descriptions of frank realities, including some harsh ones. But the narration shows, always, the positive counterpoint of humanity.

The scenery is diverse. It places before the eyes of the reader, encouraged and curious, abruptly rising peaks and immense green plains, which gradually move across the arid, hot, and empty vastness of the Sahara.

Huge lines of obedient camels wearing colorful blankets form unhurried caravans on roads of endless kilometers . . .

The characters are mostly rustic. In them, one finds, at times, traces of fearful kindness, as well as lack of education, of improved principles. There is also the paraphrase of legends considered sacred. Religious sentiment expressed through historic habits.

When the reader naturally wonders about the existence of a love story, the author conveys that love is present, all the stronger for being delayed. The social layers in the story become unexpectedly wrapped into the plot. The love that appears is stronger than violence and fear; it is clothed in heroism.

You have to read to see!

Maria Helena Carneiro Catunda
Member of the Academy of Letters of Belo Horizonte
Member of the Academy of Letters of Caxambu
Author of *Migrantes* (Mirto, 1998)

INTRODUCTION

John wanted to write biographies of anonymous people and prove that on the human beach every grain of sand is very valuable. Not only this, but also to unveil the mysterious power of overcoming that emanates from the courage of each person facing situations that seem insurmountable. "The situation forges the hero, not the other way around," he always said.

After telling his own story in his debut novel, *The Breath of Belief,* John waited for the right moment to return to Paris to interview the tour guide who had made a deep impression on him on his first visit to the City of Light. At the time, he was newly married to Lilly and they had engaged the services of Mádja, owner of big eyes and an unwavering smile. On their way to the Palace of Versailles, Mádja had revealed to them part of his extraordinary life story.

He had omitted, however, the most tense moments, which John heard only later when he met him again in Paris, over a coffee and a croissant. Reflective at times, with his gaze lost in the infinite, Mádja thus described his story: "A brat,

John . . . a kid! I was fifteen or sixteen years old. I saw my parents murdered. I watched as the farm where I lived literally turned to ashes. Nobody should have to deal with a situation like that at this or any other age. I was lost, desolate, with nowhere to go. Left to fate. The terrorists' bullets didn't hit my body, but they wounded my soul. After the tragedy, I remember the sun setting on the horizon, drawing the melancholy contours of that afternoon's vegetation. In the last beams of light, I saw hope resurge, swaying in misaligned camels and blue turbans. Finding the Tuareg saved me, gave me back the courage to live. It made my heart beat stronger for my first love. Maybe I would doubt my own story if I hadn't lived it. Believe it if you want to, but that's exactly how it happened."

CHAPTER 1

John arrived in Paris in the first days of March. It was cold and the icy wind, the kind that can give full purpose to scarves, reminded him of his home country, Canada. He was anxious, not just because he wanted to meet his friend again, but because he wanted to step outside his comfort zone. He felt driven to transpose his extensive academic experience into dynamic biographies. He had already written hundreds of anthropological studies and articles, which had won him awards, elevating him in the field.

He knew how to handle his cold, technical theses. Now, however, it would be different. Such publications would give way to lives and stories sealed by mystery, by the inexplicable in the light of reason.

Writing biographies, real stories, loaded with feelings and twists and turns, would be a big change, a new journey. A huge step into the unknown. He would risk his reputation as a rational researcher in an attempt to reveal the transcendental, what exists beyond intellect, beyond charts and statistics. John was not unaware of the extraordinary circumstances. There was, however, one more challenge: to describe them from his friend's point of view.

Paris without Lilly was not the same. Neither did John feel the same charm as he had on his honeymoon. The City of Light was still beautiful and elegant, and despite the early spring, it was still adorned with its white winter clothes. For him, it no longer had the intrinsic charm of the first times, nor the lively, intoxicating feeling of the celebration of love. Lilly came this time as well, but stayed only for two days before returning to Brazil, due to obligations related to her new endeavor. She was pregnant. She was carrying the fruit of a sudden, intense, and honest love. Meanwhile, John needed to start his project and wanted to do it before his son (or daughter) was born. He wanted to devote himself to the child and have time to help his wife after the birth.

John stayed in the same hotel where they had been on her honeymoon, in the southern part of the city, which made vivid recollection of the good times they had spent there. Everything brought back memories: the sober and elegant decoration, the excellent service, the soft scent of a unique fragrance ordered by the hotel and delicately sprinkled in the environment. A purposeful déjà vu, which made sense, since

John's interviewee worked out of this hotel and thus would be more conveniently found.

As he waited in the immense and sumptuous hall, John watched the shuffle of tourists immersed in the romantic and seductive air of the city, as he once had been. His eyes sparkled, remembering the good time he had spent there. *Never to forget*, he thought.

He disconnected from the incessant fuss, wondering how he should begin the interview and what points would serve as the basis for his second book. As he reflected, he saw, in the distance, the unmistakable smile of Mádja. His friend had changed his appearance. His hair was now shorter and he no longer had a beard, looking even younger than the last time they met. He finished off his cool-chic look with a pair of boots that were a natural complement to his tight pants ripped at the knee. An unbuttoned overcoat indicated that the cool temperature did not bother him so much. Instead of a handshake, they greeted each other with a tight, warm hug, typical of great friends—a moment that made it clear that we don't always need words to break the silence (so much can be said within a hug!). Sometimes a conversation, an encounter, first happens in the soul.

After countless virtual contacts, this was only the second time they met in person. It was one of those timeless friendships that neither need to be tried nor need daily contact to develop. They neither need the fire of suffering, nor the lightness of joys to be forged. They are born from the heart and are rare, like a red diamond.

Mádja stepped back and, before John could say anything, said, "Mr. Moore! How nice to see you again! I hope I didn't keep you waiting too long. Shall we go to the restaurant? I've learned that you can't have a good conversation on an empty stomach."

"My friend Mádja! Please, call me John. And it's my pleasure to see you again. You must tell me how time passes and yet you manage to look even younger. Of course you know the chef. Who don't you know in Paris? Ha! Ha! And I accept your suggestion. Let's eat and talk. What is special is to be able to meet you again here and to have the chance to write your story."

"If you go out I think you will need a coat. That won't do," said Máda, pointing to John's T-shirt. "You are Canadian, but you have lived in Brazil for so long that you must be out of the habit. I know the chef at the hotel and told him we would have a very special guest today!" He smiled.

"Oh, Mádja, my bones don't forget the Toronto winter. Almost thirty years of throwing snowballs, skiing, and living a normal life in minus thirty degrees," John replied. "Do you know what it is like to spend months living in a temperature below thirty, forty degrees?"

"I don't know and I don't want to know. What I have here is cold enough," he replied, his smile widening.

During lunch, John clarified the reason for his wife's absence, which made his friend happy. The news of the pregnancy and that everyone was doing well created a relaxed and even friendlier atmosphere. Little by little, the author's nervousness disappeared. They confirmed their schedules and chose where they would meet, and John explained how he would like to write. He would write down the main facts and embellish with fiction. Mádja had no objections. He trusted his friend, and something told him that John would know how to write the story well.

CHAPTER 2

The next day, John arrived early at the appointed place. He went in, ordered a coffee, and fed his writer's reverie by remembering that Hemingway, the Fitzgeralds, T. S. Eliot, Saint-Exupéry, and so many other authors had also been there. Hemingway, coincidentally, had lived in Toronto (the city where John grew up) before Paris. Maybe Hemingway had sat in this same chair, in exactly the same place as him. Maybe he'd also enjoyed a macchiato, as John was drinking. Unfortunately, none of this would make John write like Hemingway, or any of those great writers from the past. He would have to walk his own path, roll the stones with his own strength, following only his instinct. There could be no place more inspiring than the cafés that echoed the French Belle Époque. At John's request, they would take turns, day after day, talking in the various historic places on Boulevard Saint-Germain. John opted to pay a little more for the charm and history that, as a bonus, gave him a good cup of coffee and a croissant.

Once Mádja arrived, he ordered his breakfast and, as they ate, he began to recapitulate his life. His birth in Ghana, his parents' daydreaming in search of diamonds in Sierra Leone, and their escape from civil war in search of tranquility in Ivory Coast. He spoke fondly about the years of peace and stability on the cocoa farm outside Yamoussoukro and the positive impact of the French mission on his education. He abandoned his smile when he recounted the tragic death of his parents, murdered by cowardly local extremists, and his escape to North Africa in the company of Tuareg. Difficult memories, which were overcome by faith and the single-minded desire for others to be fed the eternal bread of mercy and forgiveness. Mádja lingered the longest on his journey into the unknown to the north and his encounter with the Tuareg, one of the most interesting and unique peoples on the planet. John captured the power of that time in his life.

The year in which his friend was lost in the north of the country would be the main subject of the book. John knew a little about the Tuareg and his curiosity as an anthropologist spoke loudly.

John started to record and put his little notebook on the table. He liked to take notes even as he recorded the conversation, writing down random ideas in pen as they came into his mind. This system allowed him to jot down details that stood out to him while not missing anything in his friend's narrative. He asked Mádja to keep talking, because he was not going to interrupt him.

The adventure to West Africa, to nowhere, to nothingness. Thus began John's research for his second biographical novel.

CHAPTER 3

That seemed to be another year of calm, of normality, like any other year. The French mission school on the farm had finished its term and we were on vacation, helping with the chores. That week, we had finished preparing the cocoa to be shipped to the city.

I was a big fan of the Brazilian soccer team that had won the 1994 World Cup in the United States. Romário was my great idol, but I wore the jersey of the young Ronaldo, who was about my age at the time and just starting to become famous. We organized a soccer match on the farm, on a makeshift dirt field, with a ball that one of the missionaries had brought from France. This new official World Cup ball was the big attraction of the game, and of course I couldn't wait to try it out.

It was late afternoon, and just before the game started, we were interrupted by the arrival of a small entourage consisting of a white priest, a young black man, and a strange man in a black turban with a cloth covering his face so that only his eyes showed. They were each mounted on camels loaded with handicrafts, apricots, and other delicacies that they intended to sell or exchange for cocoa.

The priest was dressed funny, in a brown habit tied with a dirty rope around his waist and a wooden cross hanging on his chest. Thin and withered, he looked like a white monkey. We laughed at him without even disguising it. He didn't seem to mind either.

He knew the religious missions in the region and used his contacts to help the Tuareg with their business dealings in the farms, towns, and villages they passed through. The young black man, a few years older than me, much shorter and thinner, caught my attention. He had one arm much thinner than the other, which, besides the obvious aesthetic difference, made him walk in a curious way, swinging only his good arm. That figure with the veil, on the other hand, was a bizarre sight. The turban, the sword, the deep and mysterious expression. It was like a mirage that did not dissipate in the desert heat, like a character out of an old book or a Hollywood movie.

The owner of the farm received the entourage with joy, for he seemed to like the fruit and collected exotic and rare handicrafts. The group stopped next to the soccer field and watched as the match was about to begin. We counted the players and, in the absence of one, invited the young black man to join in, since the priest and the Tuareg didn't seem to understand the game. He accepted, without blinking. I think that was all he wanted, because he responded to the invitation even before we finished asking.

He joined my team, and although he could run well, he was awkward and unbalanced because of his arm. He played next to me and kept passing the ball to me, telling me to shoot straight at the goal.

Even at the age of fifteen, I stood out. It might have been Ronaldo's shirt, or an innate ability that I received from who knows where, because though my father was a tough defender who would even beat his mother if she dribbled him, he had never scored. The difference in skill between me and the rest of the boys on the field was so great that as soon as the ball touched my feet, my body did the rest. I dribbled, ran, and used my uncommon physical strength. I protected the ball and carried it toward the goal and shot with my left foot, my fatal weapon. Four to one, victory for my team. For the second time in a row, I was the star of the annual game that marked the end of the working season on the farm. You cannot imagine how it filled me up. A simple game, but I played so well that I was happy for several days, reliving every shot, surprised at myself for having managed to do it.

The newcomer approached me after the game. "Hey, you play very well! I'm Abdar, nice to meet you. What is your name?"

"Mádja. Thanks. I'm going to be a soccer player. There's a missionary who will help me go to France next year."

"Nice! You've got the makings of a real player. You're tall for your age and good. Players like you are valued these days. You have to be strong to play soccer, skill is not enough, and you've got both. We're going to North Africa, it's gonna take us months with these damned camels, but we're going," Abdar said jokingly. "If you want, you can come with us, and from there we can go to Europe."

"Thanks, but I'd prefer to go by plane, it's a little faster," I laughed. "When I first saw some of them passing overhead, I was scared, but one day I want to be on one of them."

The small entourage concluded their exchanges and business dealings with the farm owner, and Abdar said goodbye, predicting again that I would be a soccer star in the future.

They turned off the main road in the late afternoon until they lined up with a light that could be seen in the distance. It was the caravan camp, where they would regroup. I followed them with my eyes until I lost sight of them.

*_*_*

At the farm, everyone was looking forward to receiving the dividends of the fruit of all their hard work and sweat. We separated the cocoa into different piles, one for each buyer, and defined who would make the deliveries. Once the hardest part of the work was over, we could feel in the air a relief and happiness of mission accomplished. As usual, Dominic, the owner of the farm, ordered a celebration, enhanced with good food, music, and dancing. The day was special and every year, after the soccer match, the moment was like an early Christmas dinner.

The cooks worked on *kedjounou*, a kind of stew with tomato, onion, and local chili seasoning. This was accompanied by fried cassava and banana, tomato rice, and toasted ground cassava. The food was the highlight of the feast and celebration. At the end of that night, we went to sleep happy, with a sense of accomplishment, and ready to fulfill our annual goal the next day in Yamoussoukro.

Sunday morning began with the preparations for the cocoa delivery. Early in the morning, we were all on our feet, each with his or her well-defined role. A large table was set up in the courtyard to serve breakfast with bread, scrambled eggs, butter, and goat cheese. To drink, coffee and mint tea. The purpose was that we could all eat together and socialize before leaving.

I ate something quick and, at the farm owner's request, went to investigate a leak in the roof of the main house. I always made myself useful. I had learned to repair various machines and structures by accompanying my father. My parents had taught me from an early age the value of work. I was always available for any task.

On the way, I watched the shuttle of workers. I couldn't hide my desire to go to the city with my parents, but on those days, I had to stay on the farm to help. There was too much work and not enough labor, since most of the employees were busy delivering cocoa.

The morning started out hot and humid, and although I was already familiar with the weather, I felt that the day was heavy. There was something hovering in the air. Something that you cannot specify, but that you know is not good. Ignoring the unusual intuition, I went on with my task, climbing on the roof and heading for the leak.

As I walked, I stared at the horizon and admired the wide, clear view of the morning. From above, the sight of the same landscape I saw every day changed. I thought the region was beautiful, but from above it became fascinating. It was in this almost trancelike state that I heard a dry crack. It sounded strange, but I concluded that it was the sound of a gunshot. *An accident*, I thought to myself.

Several more shots, in sequence, made me sure that it was no accident. With my heart racing, I bent down, out of reflex, and walked as carefully as I could, trying to see what was going on. What happened next changed my life forever.

CHAPTER 4

I looked inside the main courtyard and witnessed the brutal execution of some of the workers. I knew that among them were my parents. It is impossible to recall all the details of what one feels at such a moment. It is a mixture of the worst sensations that manifest physically, like an emotional bomb.

I was breathing short and fast. My whole body was tingling, and I was walking with difficulty. It was as if the path that I had overcome with ease suddenly became twisting, full of obstacles. My heart seemed to explode in my chest. Dizzy and balancing with difficulty, I wanted to run, but my knees failed me. I doubted my own eyes. I swallowed a cry of pain, felt a twinge of despair, and just remember babbling, "Mom! Dad!"

* * *

Mádja stretched out his hand towards Boulevard Saint-Germain as he recalled the moment. He watched the movement of people, ignoring the commotion and reexperiencing, perhaps, the murder of his parents. There was a real expression of pain on his face, perhaps the same one he had made almost twenty years ago, watching the whole thing from the roof of the farm. He brought his hand to his mouth, as if he didn't want to speak anymore, but he took a deep breath, excused himself, and continued.

* * *

We were surprised by terrorists, without having even a second to react. Cowardice, wanton cruelty. I looked to one of the corners of the courtyard, saw my mother lying there, taking her last breath. She was looking for me, her eyes glazed. Even today that look is imprinted in my memory. Sometimes the image comes out of nowhere, no matter if I am listening to rock 'n' roll or cooking fish for friends. It simply appears in my mind and takes me, like a skillful robber waiting for the right moment to strike and to remind us never to let our guard down.

My mother had been shot and she was leaning against the wall, right at the corner of the yard. I guess she was searching for me, when our eyes met. She looked relieved for a second. She reached out her arm, as if to touch me, and whispered with difficulty, "Save yourself, my son." I could read her lips from afar. She closed her eyes for the last time and perhaps took comfort in the possibility that I might make it out alive.

I was trying to understand what could not be understood. I was trembling, listening to my heartbeat. I could barely feel my body and I wanted to climb off the roof, to shake my mother and father, to wake them up, to get out of a nightmare.

Between shock and dread, I fought against the pleas of my body and knew that I had to keep quiet because I was in grave danger. *They're going to kill me, they're going to kill me*, was all I could think.

If I was found, I would also be branded a traitor and murdered, as the others had been. They spared no one. Crying silently and hiding on the roof, I could hear the terrorists screaming hysterically, slapping their tongues on the roof of their mouth. They had gone mad because of that bloody revenge. An unfounded cruelty of man against man.

They displayed the farm owner's body like a trophy, stripped naked and riddled with countless bullets. The whole thing lasted no more than thirty or forty minutes, but it seemed like countless hours to me. Despite the whirlwind of emotions, I had to act.

CHAPTER 5

On the roof, I was trying to process a myriad of new and terrifying emotions. At the same time, I had to think about how to remain hidden. I asked the God that the French mission had taught me to believe in, *Why? Why that? Why us?*

I believe that my mother, with her last words, saved me, because I focused on her dying wish that I get out of there alive.

These terrorists invaded the land of those who traded with the French. They were nationalists, opposed to the presence of anyone related to France. They destroyed everything, burning buildings and crops, leaving a trail of blood and hatred behind them. They shouted "Death to traitors" in a histrionic frenzy. Every word, every sound they uttered was like a blade piercing my soul. I cried quietly, trying not to make any noise.

I watched their movements as they searched the house for valuables. Later, I found out that they were going to sell them to raise money for the cause they were defending with all their might. Once the action was over, they headed towards the capital, where they would plan their next attack. The last two to leave poured gasoline on everything and set fire to the courtyard before running off at high speed on a motorcycle.

Before the fire reached the main building, I escaped through a rugged shortcut, taking advantage of my youth and knowledge of the place. I walked away from the farm and saw, in the distance, everything collapsing. I climbed a hill, from where I could get a wider view. I looked in all directions for help. My family, my beloved farm, my friends, in ruins right before me. And I'd done nothing. I'd watched that hateful massacre of dozens of innocent souls, amid the dark smoke rising in the sky.

I repeated, clapping my hands against my head, "Why us? Why us?" as if repeating these questions would give me any answers.

I remember it as if it were today. I wanted to find a reason for what had happened. The truth is that there is nothing that justifies cruelty.

There was no town, no neighboring farm, or anything in the vicinity where I could go. I found refuge in the shade of a tree. I felt exhausted, as if I had played ten soccer matches in a row.

I sat down, leaning against a tree, and cried like never before. Abandoned by hope, I stared at the farm—or what was left of it. I relived that moment. My mother's last look of despair was burned into my soul. The next few hours are hazy in my mind, but I either slept or passed out, I am not sure. I got up at dusk and, standing up, I saw in the distance what was to be my salvation.

CHAPTER 6

On the horizon, tearing through the colors of the twilight, I saw a large convoy. I remembered the entourage that had visited us the day before the attack. Since camels were rare in that region, it could only be them. I ran, feeling my body's strength returning. I approached the caravan. I realized that they had stopped. In places where they didn't negotiate, they let the animals rest and slept leaning against them to speed up their departure the next day.

At a safe distance, I laid down my aching body, trying not to be noticed. I took turns between watching them and planning my approach the next morning.

I looked up at the stars that I had once thought so beautiful. I lost, for a moment, the ability to see the resonance of the Creator. The proclamation of what is divine in everything, the innate sonority of all that connects us. I began to experience a mental numbness, as if I couldn't react to the situation. I focused on surviving and trying to find Abdar, the boy who'd played soccer with me on the farm. While I was waiting for a more opportune moment, I fell asleep, exhausted by the tension of what had happened.

In the early-morning hours, I was awakened by a curious lizard that was seeking shelter under the same rock I was sleeping on. We exchanged a few glances, then ignored each other. We both had more important things to do. I kept an eye on the caravan's movements from afar and had the idea of turning my blue shirt into a false turban, imitating the travelers, leaving only my eyes exposed.

Sneaking up on them, I joined them and passed oblivious to the eyes of those who, I would later learn, were in the upper castes. I held back my tears, swallowed the anger, which came in waves, and followed my instinct. I was fighting for my life to honor my mother's last wish. I did not know what language the members of the caravan spoke, let alone where they were going. I followed my strange friends into the unknown. I looked for Abdar and moved to a part of the caravan where there were people with darker skin like mine. They traveled on foot, using their camels to carry handicrafts, fruit, and salt.

The pain of the loss of my parents wounded me like the tip of a dagger. And with each step, I felt it. I began to perceive the calls of my body. The hunger and thirst that I had forgotten about came back to haunt me. I weakened and my legs insisted on not obeying me. Finally, I recognized Abdar, with his peculiar gait, as if he were carrying only one side of his body. I approached him and said in a low voice, "Hey, Abdar. Hey!"

"Yeah," he said, turning to me, perhaps imagining that I was someone from the caravan. "Ah! The footballer! Mádja, isn't it? What are you doing here, kid?"

"They attacked the farm. No one else survived. I need help. I don't know what to do," I said, trusting the only person in the world I knew at that moment. "I have nowhere to go and I don't want to be alone."

"Who attacked you? And Dominic? And his parents?" he asked with surprise.

"I don't know who attacked us," I said, catching my breath. "Everybody was killed. Shot, burned. I escaped by miracle."

After saying these words, I cried in an uncontrollable way. Abdar looked at me tenderly and told me to change my turban, as the color black would be more appropriate for our caste. Guessing my need, he hugged me, under curious glances, which soon turned away.

I discovered, a short time later, that the people in that part of the caravan had learned centuries ago to take care of their own lives. They had already carried too many tragedies on their shoulders to worry about others.

Abdar recognized himself in me and gave me the support he'd never received.

"I escaped from a diamond mine and joined the caravan two months ago, not unlike you, Mádja. You can count on me, I will help you. If you keep quiet and help with the work, no one will bother you. Unfortunately, stories like ours are common in this part of the country."

"Thank you, Abdar. Who are these people? I have never seen anything like this."

"They're the Kel Ahaggar Tuareg. They're from Assekrem, which means 'end of the world.' Scary, isn't it? They're very traditional. I heard that they've gathered a large stock of handicrafts, salt, and other products and decided to trade them in Niger, Burkina Faso, and Ivory Coast, looking for new markets and buying supplies. They still talk about a big drought in the last years, when animals and people got sick and died. They needed to walk to survive, I was told."

"Like me, now. Walking to survive," said Mádja, as he looked at the front of the caravan, which was starting to move away.

"Yes, walking is necessary, Footballer. They suffered from the losses of the various civil wars in which they fought for respect, for the recognition of a Tuareg territory. That's all I've heard. As for destination, they seem to be going home now. I don't understand their language. And the Haratin and *iklan*, whom we are now walking with, are not given this information. These people are not even considered Tuareg! They are supposed to serve them, travel around, following them and doing the heavier work. They also have small business in the shadows," Abdar added.

"Great! We're on the run, with no family and nothing, in the last position of a caravan of strange people, heading for the end of the world. What could be better than this?"

"Do you remember the priest? The one who did business with the owner of the farm?"

"That little white guy who went with you to the farm?"

"Yep, that's the one," he smiled, confirming. "I think he is French. They accepted him and call him White Marabout, the servant of the one God, because they need someone to translate French in the negotiations. And the priest has learned Tamashek, the language of the Tuareg. You will see him again soon."

He also explained a few things to me and told me about the final destination, the city of Tamanrasset. "From there I will disconnect from the caravan and go to Rabat and then the Maghreb. I want to get to Morocco and go on to Europe," he said with a twinkle in his eyes. "There I will become rich and be able to return and help my family."

"I want the priest to help me find out who killed my parents so the police can arrest them."

"Yes, Mádja. That's what should happen. I know you are very young, but understand that here where we are, justice is a luxury."

He finished by putting his hand on my shoulder, starting a relationship that would last forever. And he indicated that we needed to start walking again.

"We are falling behind. Let's go!" said Abdar.

In silence, I clenched my teeth so hard, I remember feeling my facial muscles aching. As we ran to catch up, I breathed through my mouth in short, rapid rhythms, and soon I was tired. I frowned and swallowed, remembering why my parents had agreed to work on the farm. Peace. It was everything they'd dreamed of. They'd wished for peace and received a cruel and torpid death.

I reached for the goatskin *gherba* at Abdar's waist, abusing the newly made friendship, and drank some of his water. I took the only course of action that was right for me at that moment—I moved forward.

CHAPTER 7

With the curtain of naivety open, Mádja lived one step at a time. He put his pieces back together, like everyone who for the first time comes into contact with the tragic face of existence.

The caravan traveled for many hours along the Bandama Valley. They came across small dams, full of greenery and various species of birds. The soft and refreshing breeze, the rain that visited them every day in the afternoon. The Tuareg, masters of the sands of the Sahara, as they called themselves, delighted in these days. They liked the sensations brought by the rain, like the light touch of moisture on the skin, to rub their fingers and already feel them wet. The anticipation of the drops, the smell of wet earth. The sound of water meeting the ground, which for the Tuareg, the inhabitants of the desert, represented the sound of life.

On the outskirts of the city of Bouaké, they took the opportunity to do business and set up camp. In the places where they intended to sell more and deepen commercial relations, they stopped and pitched tents, the frames of which would remain there for future trips. They dressed them in leather and, in this way, formalized the camp. The ritual was the confirmation that they would stop there for at least a week.

* * *

Abdar soon called me to help with the work, warning that I could not deny the task if I wanted to remain unnoticed. I joined him and was soon amazed at the elegance of the Tuareg. Tall and slender, with strong black eyes. I stared at the characteristic *tagelmust*, the dark-blue turban, dyed from fermented indigo leaves. I couldn't help but notice the Tuareg's tanned skin, in a bluish tone, the result of the depigmentation of the veil, which gave them the nickname "the blue men." Wide pants, tied with a tucked-in leather belt, completed the outfit. For the ancient lords of the desert, blue was the color of the world. It was the color of everything. It was the color of their celestial roof. It was not the black veil of the lower castes, but rather the showy, long blue cloth that completed the mystical aura of these legendary people.

One of the leaders of the group dismounted from his camel, picked up a clump of dirt, and rubbed it between his hands. There was, surrounding his presence, a tension that did not exist in the modern world. He seemed ready for a fight at any moment, to defend his honor in a fatal combat. Maybe it was just my boyish impression. Anyways, he approached me and, ignoring my presence, tied up his camel. It was the first time I felt invisible. The camel, yes, this one was looking at me, with a stupid face, chewing on some branch. It had light skin and dark spots under its eyes. I learned later that it was a mehari, a docile and intelligent breed. Considered to be the most resistant to the adversities of the desert. This particular animal had won several races in the legendary city of Timia and was worth a lot to its owner. It was adorned with showy multicolored blankets, which separated its body from its pen.

It was then that the Tuareg's penetrating gaze crossed mine. A different look. I noticed, on the spot, that he thought he was superior, perhaps the fruit of years and years of slavery of the lower castes, which, at that moment, I didn't understand. I tried to conceal my curiosity about the unknown. All I needed was to remain incognito.

CHAPTER 8

John remembered a class with his favorite anthropology professor. John had written every word he said down and catalogued it for future reference. He did a search on his computer and found a short transcript about the Tuareg that said, "The word *Tuareg* is a Bedouin Arabic name that originally designated the inhabitants of Fezzan, in southern Libya. The Tuareg, descendants of the warrior queen Tin Hinan, are divided into castes. The nobles and the warriors are the *imajeren*, 'the proud and free.' They capture slaves, *iklan*, who become a part of Tuareg society and families, with opportunities to change their status through marriage and devotion."

Happy with his find, he told Mádja about it as soon as he arrived at the café. Some attributes of the Tuareg were unknown to his friend, who had lived the experience in his own skin but did not know all these historical details.

The writer was amazed at the courage of Mádja, who, still a boy, had decided to enter that caravan without even knowing where they were going. Mádja agreed, adding that courage is a close friend of youthful impetus.

* * *

That first night with them, I finished my work and had a piece of cheese with bread and goat butter. I drank some mint tea, which brought a quick sense of comfort, since it was something I was used to. I walked away from Abdar, who was expertly baking a loaf of bread on an improvised firepit, thanking him for the snack. I lay down in a makeshift tent, made of rubble and plastic bags, and out of nowhere I began to cry. An abnormal crying, a mental pain that manifested itself, like anguish, in my chest. I spent the night alternating between periods of light sleep, fear, and nightmares, in which I relived the scenes of the tragedy.

It is difficult to pinpoint the moment. Many details have blurred with the passage of time. It has been almost twenty years now. I think I was experiencing absolute isolation, a quiet desperation. In the early nights, I was plagued by the apparent meaninglessness that surrounded my life. That space created in the soul that can only be filled with a prayer, you know?

* * *

John knew. He had suffered from the death of his parents in a car accident years ago and the near death of his wife in an episode shortly after their marriage. Lilly had had an allergic crisis and been saved by a miracle. In these hours, the mind closes and the soul opens. One feels the lance of reality, cruel and painful, in the submission of the will to the hard test, in the poverty evidenced by the mind's incapacity in the face of mystery. The revelation of our vulnerability, which, even though it is a precondition for love, opens two paths for us: one that leads us to bitterness and the other, which makes us heroes.

"Mádja, my friend. I want you to know that I have not interrupted you because I respect your story and I want to let you follow your narrative. Do not think, however, that I don't feel when I hear the barbarities that you have witnessed. I know what it is to lose one's parents. I am sorry for what you have been through."

"John, I understand. Thank you."

Between sips of coffee, Mádja remembered difficult moments. Not without pain, but without the self-pity of those who suffer for suffering's sake. There was a nobility in the way he dealt with these facts. They were wounds that still bothered, but seemed already organized, healed. Mádja cited the strong influence of Christian teachings in the way he dealt with suffering. He cherished the long conversations with his father, from which he drew precious lessons of a simple man who never accepted victimization. In adult life, by luck, fate, or both, he found a friend-father, who, besides being his mentor, helped him by showing him the importance of talking to a professional about his worst moments and creating mechanisms to deal with the consequences. Still, he suffered from difficulty in maintaining relationships, a chronic difficulty sleeping, and devastating feelings of shame and guilt that surfaced when he least expected them.

John was sure that there was, in the memories of his friend, evidence of an invisible bridge that allowed people to transcend the ordinary, that lifted them to a point where they could overcome any limits. There was his friend, smiling, making the best of his life, despite all that he had suffered. This was the tone of the stories John wanted to tell.

CHAPTER 9

Mádja finished his meeting with John and, after seeing a client, he went back to his apartment. After years on a television show traveling around the country, he'd managed to use the money he had saved to buy his own two-bedroom apartment, one bedroom of which he rented out to supplement his income. The tenant, Elena, a Swiss architect, was the daughter of Antony, Mádja's partner and his boss from his TV days. He was Mádja's mentor, who had helped him so much, leading him to seek treatment and counseling to deal with his traumas.

Elena had grown up on the road with her father, who would go from town to town recording his television show. She'd met Mádja when he worked for the show and they became friends. She was a lovely person, easy to get along with. Mádja was happy to have her around, but that day after meeting with John, he was grateful that she had gone on vacation. He needed some time to be alone.

Elena's good taste was reflected in every corner of the almost hundred-square-meter apartment, located thirty minutes away from the center of Paris. From the apartment, Mádja could walk to the Seine and contemplate the landscape, which he did regularly. There was not much nature to see, but there is something about watching the running water that enchants those who meditate, contemplate, and try to empty their minds. The building was old, like almost everything else in Paris and its surroundings, but the open concept of the unit, together with its decoration, gave the interior a very modern feel.

When Mádja arrived home that night, before entering, he stopped for a moment. He took a deep breath and sighed loudly, right in front of the big double door, made of hardwood and painted with varnish. After a few seconds, he entered, ignoring his hunger and going straight to the bar in the right corner. There was a bench and three high chairs. He chose the last one to sit down in. He opened a wine he had been given by a customer, without noticing that it was a Corton-Bressandes Grand Cru.

The wine was expensive and very well rated. Mádja drank the entire bottle, unceremoniously and even without noticing the characteristic bouquet of black currant and raspberry. That was one of his favorite corners in the house, just below a huge framed poster of a French rock band from the 1970s called Téléphone. Sitting there, he looked out the window, staring at the street. He was like someone who, through a fixed point, remembers the past and imagines what life would be like if everything had happened differently.

CHAPTER 10

In the cold Parisian morning the next day, John met with Mádja to write new chapters of his unique life story. At the door of the café, the first customers of the day exchanged a few words before entering and looking for a corner table in the window.

"Good morning, my friend. Did you sleep well?" asked John.

"More or less, my friend. Getting a good night's sleep is already a rare event for me. But remembering the events, it has become more complicated," Mádja replied, smiling.

"I can imagine. We'll go at your pace. When you need to take a break, or anything else, let me know."

John noticed his friend's tired eyes. He entered the café first and pointed in the direction of where he wanted them to sit.

Sitting down, waiting for the waiter, John reinforced the Canadian reputation for being polite and always apologetic. "I am sorry to cause you any grief."

"Don't be sorry, my friend. There is no way to look at our scars without remembering the events that caused them," Mádja pointed out.

They settled into the soft upholstered chairs and resumed their work. Mádja picked up the narrative where he had left off.

* * *

The twilight preceding the mornings was the harbinger of a full day. Physically and mentally exhausted, I had overslept. It was strange, because on the other nights I persistently relived the nightmare of my parents' death and my mother's final gaze.

Abdar, who was in the next tent, nudged me with a stick. He told me to help him prepare the food and join the Tuareg who were selecting the goods that would be negotiated in the next village. We prepared couscous and milked the goats. The Tuareg woke up very early. They ate in the morning and then again only when we stopped, at the end of the day. The first meal was strong, to support the daily journey, which could reach sixteen hours of marching and cover up to fifty kilometers in one day. After breakfast, they would carefully check the water reserves and then leave. They had an almost military routine that was repeated every day.

Abdar and I were immersed in this hard reality. And there we were walking under the reddish color of dawn. We had no choice. The subcastes, of which we were a part, were in charge of the heavy work. We transported the traded goods and stored them as ordered by the *imageren*. We also took care of the animals and made sure the women and the children had water. I felt weak. I was not in the habit of eating so little and working so hard.

Abdar, already used to it, helped me a lot and, little by little, we built our friendship, forged by the hardships we shared. He rarely got tired. Even the problem with his arm did not hinder him. Abdar had a thin face with wide ears. He looked and was very funny. He had a witty sense of humor, with jokes that were easy to understand, but at the same time, he could surprise me with deep phrases, evidence that he knew the serious side of life. It was a mixture that made me want to be next to him. Though I didn't have a brother, Abdar was the person who came closest to this relationship for me.

In suffering, in pain, the development of a friendship seems to cut paths.

The work and the conversations with Abdar distracted me from the memories that stubbornly stole my attention when I was at rest. In the last moments of the night, my body, even though tired, allowed my mind to travel for a few seconds before falling asleep. Sleep was the result of overwork, but sleep did not relieve the pain or restore my energy. The dawn was painful in every way. I thought that because I was young and played soccer every day, I would not feel tired. Not at all! My muscles remembered every effort, every new movement, as if I were a sedentary person starting a weight-training program. None of this mattered, because in the rigid regime, nobody complained or asked anything.

We had arrived in Bouaké and camped there for a couple of days. The Tuareg ended up staying longer than originally planned. That was when I recognized the unusual interpreter-priest, the "white monkey," as we had called him, who translated all the negotiations, preventing the Tuareg from being cheated. As I helped the upper castes, I approached those of the caravan considered the most noble.

I noticed with surprise that most of the children, as well as some of the women, spoke fluent French and Arabic. These were the ones who'd gone to the school that served the Assekrem region. The men, however, spoke only the Tuareg language. They refused to learn French. Since only the men could trade, the priest was an essential presence.

The help of an interpreter within the group allowed the income to be multiplied by the lack of intermediaries. As Abdar helped me to get involved with important tasks, I was always close to the priest. Once or twice, the priest's gaze crossed mine, but he did not speak a word to me. I was waiting patiently for the right moment to approach him. My interest in meeting him was growing. I thought or invented that he could help me find the bandits who had attacked the farm and then help me get to Europe to play soccer, so I focused on that.

In the meantime, Abdar kept repeating his dream of going to Europe and getting rich. He had his secrets, his mysteries, and there was a good part of his story that he had not yet confided to me. I respected his silence, as he respected mine.

At the end of that day, the Tuareg concluded their negotiations in the city, and so, at first light, we planned to return to the road once more. Before going to sleep, however, a man who claimed to represent the city's buyers appeared in the camp, bringing an offer the desert people could not refuse.

CHAPTER 11

Salomon Koné, the man from the city, was an amiable-looking fellow with a wide smile and gray hair. A little chubby and with a few missing teeth, he insisted that the Tuareg stay a little longer. He had been amazed at the quality of the handicrafts. The technique used in the artwork was very rare and unique to that Tuareg tribe.

The Tuareg then invited him to tea, and together they sat around a firepit. I watched the whole thing, like a movie. The rituals meant a lot to this tribe and they lived to preserve them. One of the chiefs prepared the drink, an exclusive duty of the men. Always three jugs, and in the last one they used a curious herb to drive away the evil spirit that brings bad luck, sickness, and even death.

The tea ceremony had its history and its purpose. Then I learned, in the conversations I came to have with the priest—he knew everything about everything, or, at least, that's how I remember him—in this tea ceremony, the Tuareg determined who the guest was. They analyzed his expressions, his intentions. They liked Koné and soon began to tell the stories of the lost caravans, of those that sank in the quicksand and of those that numbered up to fifty thousand camels. Resuming the negotiations, they let the guest finally speak his proposal for trade.

Koné's offer pleased the priest, but the translation did not please the Tuareg. Koné wished them to stay a little longer in the region. The trader would provide the raw material for the women to produce an extra batch of handicrafts. Koné even proposed paying a little more. The tourists had bought all the pieces in less than a day at the town fair. The priest tried to convince the Tuareg, but without success.

Despite the good offer, they wanted to continue their journey to Mali. After months on the road, they wanted to return to the region of their ancestors. Koné insisted that they at least accept a gift. And that they promise to return the following year. He told the Tuareg that he would send a surprise to celebrate the new trade alliance they had started.

I listened to everything and was fascinated by the way the Tuareg acted and led their lives. So, I attended many discussions with the excuse of being ready to serve them in case they needed someone to carry something or do some heavy lifting. This way I kept myself busy, which helped me to survive.

Hours later, a traditional dance group came to the camp to fulfill Koné's promise. Abdar positioned himself next to me and we shared some spiced tea he'd traded for in town. We watched the dance begin just behind the line formed by the Tuareg seated as guests of honor at this performance. I watched in astonishment, seeing the vivid colors of the dancers and hearing the intoxicating beat of the drums. Plumes, straws, and cloths filled the costumes. The *moko jumbies*, dancers on stilts standing four or five meters above the ground, turned and moved their legs to the rhythm of the drums. They had painted their bodies and wore masks. Driven by the music, they enraptured the audience with their enthusiasm. That's when I felt a weight on my shoulder, pulling me out of that momentary trance. It was the priest.

CHAPTER 12

Mádja finally met the priest, or rather, was met by him. All his hope was pinned on that strange figure, whom the boy himself had made fun of on the farm when he first saw him. Gentle and moving slowly, with thoughtful and purposeful gestures, the priest approached when the Tuareg were busy dancing.

* * *

"Hello, young man. Finally, we can introduce ourselves. My name is Olaf Huber, but you can call me Brother Olaf. Aren't you the good footballer we saw at the farm?" he asked, sitting down next to me. "Do your parents know that you are with us?"

"The rebels murdered my parents," I answered. I took a deep breath. "They killed everyone. Now I have nothing and no one."

I held back the tears and swallowed hard. I tried to be strong and kept going. "I hope you can help me find out who did this to my parents and bring them to justice. Then I want to go to Europe and become a professional footballer. These are the only things that matter to me now."

Olaf asked Abdar to bring him something to eat. He sat down and, with a gesture, invited me to do the same. He lightly touched my arm and said, "I see your suffering. You've been through a lot so far, and you're still young. The world is unfair. But look, I assure you that there is a way above all this. Not a peace without struggle, but peace in the midst of struggle, beyond tragedy. Your tears are counted, my brother. As for your requests, they are difficult to fulfill. I promise, however, that when I stop in the next town, I will see what I can find out about what happened, and I will tell you." He looked deep into my eyes.

I could tell he cared. He didn't talk empty words as many do. He reminded me of the French mission priests, though I didn't understand why he was in this caravan.

"You talk like the priest from the Christian mission who taught on the farm. But you walk with the Tuareg, who don't seem to be Christians."

"They are not Christians. Far from it. However, judgment creates distance and separation and that keeps us from being with others. It is love that creates unity in me. Christianity is about others! I am with the Tuareg because I follow the philosophy of Charles de Foucauld's order, that of bringing Christ to those who do not yet know him. And by serving them, as I do, I am serving God in the same way I would in any community. Don't you agree?"

"I don't know. I don't understand anything more about God," I replied, revealing my struggle with faith since my escape from the farm tragedy. "I feel only anger and fear."

"It is normal to feel that way after what happened to you. But listen, young man, the cure for this is not to feel like a victim. You need to conquer that monster and embody it. Having courage is not the same thing as not being afraid."

He smiled trying to calm me down and I processed all this information, too dense for a boy of only fifteen. Somehow, however, the words echoed deep in my soul. That's when Abdar came back, staggering, interrupting our conversation, smiling in fear and taking a deep breath as if he had done something wrong. And hadn't he? He had asked for food using the priest's name, but he had also stolen a good piece of meat from the Tuareg. He had pretended to dance, excited by the presentation, and approached the place where the food was. He brought a good piece of mutton and laughed nervously, afraid that someone had seen him. The lower castes rarely ate meat and even the nobles ate it only on special occasions.

The priest promptly scolded him. It was not the first time he had done something like this. Eventually, Olaf shook his head and invited Abdar to join us, and we ended up laughing and eating the small feast, with the special seasoning of prohibition.

Around a campfire, we sat and listened to the priest's life story.

CHAPTER 13

"Charles de Foucauld! I read his biography years ago," said John. "This priest is an interesting figure among the Tuareg, in the middle of nowhere. A Christian among Muslims who do not abide by all the laws of their religion. I once had an experience that brought me closer to Christianity and today I am still a Christian, although I have moved away from formal practice."

"The priest is a character, yes. We still talk," replied Mádja. "He is elderly and has retired to an order where he is isolated, with almost no contact with anyone. We exchange letters. Now get this: believe it or not, before finding God he was a professional go-kart driver!"

"How strange!" said John, shaking his head in disbelief.

"Yes! The story is not a very happy one, but it's true. I have proof." replied Mádja.

* * *

The priest had been a go-kart driver as a teenager. He gave up after causing an accident in which his older brother died. They competed together, did everything together. They were brother-friends, united by blood and the desire to share life. Olaf, after the accident, vowed that he would never again drive a go-kart, or any vehicle. Distraught, he fell into a depression and even wanted to kill himself on several occasions. He could not bear the guilt for what had happened and the atmosphere of devastation that took over his family in the following years. During his last year of school he volunteered with some development projects in Central Africa, he returned to Europe renewed and wanting to do something meaningful with his life. He went back to school and continued his studies until he graduated as a civil engineer from the Technical University of Vienna. He worked for two years in Switzerland before embracing a project to rebuild roads and artesian wells to improve the lives of small communities in West Africa. The seed planted as a teenager blossomed and grew stronger. He spoke German, English, and French well. About twelve years before I met him, he had worked in Algeria in a dangerous region fraught with conflict between various ethnic groups.

One of the most threatened peoples was the Tuareg. This people without borders, who did not know governments or geographical separations. A complex identity that was difficult to understand. They were suffering from various civil wars and the blurring of their geographical boundaries, with practically no support. Olaf met the Little Brothers of Jesus, a congregation thought up by Father Charles de Foucauld but founded after his death, which worked with the Tuareg. He fell in love with the philosophy of the Little Brothers, and even more so with the Tuareg. He was filled with courage and, touched by a "supernatural vocation," as he said, he abandoned his promising career as an engineer and joined Foucauld's order. The Little Brothers lived in poverty and surrender and enjoyed the solitary life without ceasing to welcome the other, whoever he might be, in an unconditional way. In this way, Olaf filled the emptiness caused by the death of his brother, giving himself entirely.

Olaf became a priest and learned the Tamashek language through French-Tamashek books and dictionaries left by Foucauld. He continued to live in the vicinity of Tamanrasset. Later, he received permission from the Tuaregs to continue Foucauld's work in the Assekrem. The Assekrem is a mountainous area eighty kilometers from Tamanrasset and difficult to reach. One of the highest places in Algeria and the home of the Kel Ahaggar Tuareg.

Gradually, the priest gained the respect and trust of the Tuareg and proposed to teach them French to eliminate intermediaries during negotiations, preventing them from being exploited. He had spoken out against this trip they were on in the Ivory Coast because he knew that the region was experiencing several conflicts. Although a peace agreement was being sewn up, there was still enormous tension between the rebel groups and the governments of Niger and Mali. It didn't look like it was about to end. It was useless to try to dissuade those who were took no notice of the borders. According to the Tuareg, the world was not divisible. Caravans may not make so much sense nowadays, however, it was something they had always done and for them, a life was not complete if they were not part of a caravan that crossed the desert.

While the priest was telling us his story, I could see Abdar's frightened expression. He was excited by the explanation, and he took advantage of the first pause and began to question the priest, "But, Father, you really are crazy, aren't you? You abandoned your profession and your family to live with a strange and hostile people in the desert? I just can't understand it!"

Olaf smiled. He was very sure of his path. He seemed to know the normal doubt and disbelief that greets such a choice. But this did not diminish him, it did not seem to cause any negative feelings. He replied, overcome by the desire to show this joy and love for what he was doing, "My dear Abdar, my family is fine without me. There is nothing I can do for them at this time, except to solidify the example of the imitation of Christ. In fact, I feel closer and closer to my relatives. Brother Foucauld died in the Tuareg lands and his blood gave birth to respect for Christianity and sprouted in the infertile desert soil the fertile doctrine of the imitation of Christ. I hope that Christ can continue to give me strength so that this can be my inheritance. That this may be the image that my family will have of me when I go to be with him. That I may serve him until the end of my days and in this way I will serve my family, which ultimately is all men. The desert is not the absence of people, but the lack of distractions. This makes it possible to perceive the presence of the divine, and the solitude of the desert is transformed into an infinite space where all are welcome. But none of this is mine, nor is it easy. It is God's, given to me by him, who taught me to possess myself before I could give myself."

Amazed by Brother Olaf's story and the strength of his belief, Abdar and I said goodbye and walked to our camp. In silence, we lay down to the sound of melancholy melodies that flowed from improvised guitars made from cans, sticks, and wires. Sad moans of a people who lived just to live. Who didn't allow themselves to dream. Chained by an unbreakable bond. The incomprehensible words filled the air and, somehow, sounded like a cry of hope and utopia.

CHAPTER 14

The caravan traveled on for a few more days in the same region. The Tuareg felt they needed to return to the desert. They slowed down the pace of the march where there was more water. I think it was the collective unconscious taking advantage of every drop of easy water and abundant greenery that dominated the landscape. This gave me some idle time, walking long distances, which made it easier to remember the scenes of the tragedy I'd experienced, manifesting as a sharp pain in my chest and a suffocating anguish. I would look around and, out of the blue, think that someone was coming after me to finish the job. I couldn't relax, couldn't focus on the road, couldn't concentrate on anything. I was feeling fine, and suddenly a wave of anger came over me and I wanted to scream, to punch something, to put myself in danger. A struggle, day and night, of body and mind, doing whatever they wanted, without consulting me.

Once again we slept without setting up camp and left even earlier to get to Korhogo. There we would do some small business and gather provisions. Working took my mind away for a moment from the horrors I had witnessed.

Abdar was always trying to improve the mood of the conversations by making jokes about the strange beliefs of the Tuareg, trying to bring an instant of joy to me.

"A little camel's milk, Mádja?" he laughed, shaking the canister full of milk. "It has magical properties."

"You know I don't believe that. You drink it. Maybe magic will make your jokes better," I retorted, smiling.

We became inseparable friends during the chores, the stops to eat, and the sad and silent nights. In many situations, I saw that Abdar also cried. His nights were not so different, or better, than mine. He masked it better, perhaps, because he had been doing it longer.

Passing Korhogo, we reached Sikasso, where we were to have the next round of negotiations. The Tuareg, with no need for the Christian calendar, entered the year 1996 without realizing it. I calculated the date and remembered how happy the New Year celebrations used to be on the farm with my family, with a rich supper put on by Dominic.

That was in the past. And, despite the poignant pain of my memories, the next day, I had to walk again.

It was early morning in the camp. Between the crickets crunching and the winds howling, we heard the noise of the abrupt arrival of several cars, waking everyone up. Abdar and I, frightened, were slow to react. A voice, speaking in English that was difficult to understand, ordered everyone out of the tents. One by one, people were being searched and soon we were discovered too. Ten kids, some even younger than me, heavily armed, lined up those who belonged to our group. On the orders of a skinny, grouchy boy, we joined the others and were forced to get down on our knees at the cold aim of a rifle.

CHAPTER 15

"Waking up with a rifle pointed at your face and someone shouting at you to get out of the tent is a difficult situation to describe," said Mádja, ordering a second cup of coffee.

"I cannot even imagine, my friend. You had just lived through the greatest tragedy of your life and didn't have time to grieve. It must have brought back some things you wish you had forgotten," answered John, indicating to the waiter that he would accompany his friend for another cup of coffee.

"Not only did it bring back, John, but I physically felt what I experienced on the farm when my parents were murdered. It was the same again, the gunshots, the angry faces, and my mother looking at me. My legs were failing, my heart was beating so loud it felt like it would burst out of my chest. I was sweating profusely, and my fear was so great that I had to struggle to move."

Mádja explained to John how the soldiers looked like the terrorists who had killed his parents. Truculent, impatient, they looked like wild dogs hungry around the hunt.

"We could understand the seriousness of the situation, but not everyone understood the language. Why were those men there? What did they want? Only Abdar and I spoke English, among the people in this part of the camp."

The soldiers wore uniforms and red headbands. Dirty, they carried weapons, which in some cases seemed bigger than they were. One of them boasted that he carried a rocket launcher. It was noticeable that he thought it was great to have such a weapon in his hands. I swear that some of them were no more than ten years old. Their eyes dull, their faces scrunched up, angry at the world. Drugged, numb, and insensitive. Excessively violent, they screamed and assaulted everyone who was kneeling and unarmed. They said they were looking for the fugitives who had stolen the diamonds from a mine in Sierra Leone a little over two months ago. They wanted their stones back. And, of course, they wanted to find the thieves.

I remembered Abdar's words. Had he run away from that mining site after stealing the diamonds? Abdar was trying to control his body, which was shaking involuntarily.

Enraged, the bandits did not understand what the hostages in our camp were saying. They had clues that indicated that one of the thieves had come towards the caravan and tried to sell some of the diamonds in Niamey. They made it clear that they would kill one person at a time until we told them where the diamonds were. Abdar and I understood everything and found ourselves in a dilemma. We didn't want to say anything in English, because we would reveal that we didn't belong to the group. And if we kept quiet, we might die without having a chance to try anything.

As the soldier shouted, asking about the diamonds, I whispered to Abdar, careful not to be overheard, "Are you in on this?"

"Don't speak!" he replied, terrified. "Do you want to die?"

The militia leader, whom they called Kamara, could easily be identified by his missing left ear, where there was a hole visible from afar that sprouted amid a huge mass of burned and wrinkled skin. He wore a red beret, facing away from the scar, as if proud to show it. He smoked a cigar, and his dark glasses prevented us from seeing whom he was looking at. He had a rare aura of malice and contempt.

Kamara ordered one of the boy soldiers, whom he called Executioner, to choose someone to serve as an example. The boy cast his wicked eyes on our frightened faces and gladly discovered the panic that gripped Abdar. He pointed his rifle and ordered him to stand up, placing him in front of the group. He came around behind Abdar, who was crying and trembling. He was thinking not only of being discovered, but also of causing the death of that innocent group, he told me later. The soldier hit the barrel of the rifle on his head and shouted in English. "Where are the fucking diamonds? If nobody identifies themselves, I'm going to kill this one," he said. "And I'll kill another one every five minutes, until someone talks!"

The truculence and violence with which they treated everyone left us stunned and perplexed. A moment that defined life, because it put us face-to-face with death, without any doubt. Time passed and our situation seemed to be heading towards tragedy. Executioner rotated his fist, screwing the strap of his gun and clamping the rifle in the curve of his arm. He tilted his head a little to the side and squeezed his eyes shut. He handled the weapon with ease. He aimed at the back of Abdar's head and began to count.

I struggled with every single muscle in my body, between the paralyzing memories of my parents' tragedy and the urge to save my companion. Abdar was not just a friend, he was my only friend. A figure that represented my entire universe of people I could trust. After losing my parents, our friendship, however recent, was not only my only refuge, but also my most precious asset.

"Five, four, three..." Executioner cocked his rifle, "two..."

He steadied his arm and—

"STOP!"

A scream stopped the shot.

I had closed my eyes, faced the fear, and stood up to say "Stop!" in a courageous impulse that came from I don't know where. I opened my eyes and stared at the soldiers, who were, however, looking the other way. My scream had been muffled by the priest's shout. Olaf had come out of nowhere and, speaking louder than me, also said "Stop!" in English. He then asked the soldiers not to kill the boy. By some miracle, they did not notice me. I bent my knees, sat down on the ground again, and waited for the outcome.

CHAPTER 16

Kamara ordered one of the soldiers to bring the intercessor to him at gunpoint. Olaf showed no fear. He embodied the struggle of Charles de Foucauld, founder of his order, who'd been murdered for love of the Tuareg. Olaf drew strength from the echo of his greatest hero's actions.

The soldiers stared at the priest in strange clothes and of peculiar appearance. Very pale, thin, and withered, he was a laughingstock. There was, however, an inexplicable strength in that apparently weak man. Perhaps it was the strength of one who faces fear head on and does not cower. To the head of the group, Olaf said that this was the camp of the Kel Ahaggar Tuareg, the veiled warriors of Assekrem. That they were free men who worked for the Tuareg.

The priest's talk confused them. They knew the reputation of the fearless Tuareg warriors, who fought in wars in Mali as part of violent militias. They did not need another problem, but they were not entirely convinced. They demanded that the priest bring the head of the caravan, or he would kill everyone right there.

It was dawn in the camp when the priest returned with a group of the Tuareg *imageren*. They arrived, each on a camel, and dismounted under the confused gaze of the soldiers. The soldiers behaved as if they were facing a vision. A natural standout, the chief Tuareg, Aleck ag Farka, came to the front. He spoke for the group. He was the head of the Kel Ahaggar confederation. The few Tuareg warriors in the entourage carried rifles slung over their shoulders. They stood at a good distance from the soldiers and continued to stare at them.

At over six feet tall, Aleck embodied an almost mythological figure, commanding respect. His dark-blue veil almost touched the ground, and his blue face framed the sharp black eyes that helped reveal his leadership position. He looked at Kamara, who was slow to form an opinion about him. Aleck called to the priest and, in Tamashek, asked him to translate the conversation. He approached Kamara without fear. And, while the soldiers held up their rifles, Aleck saluted the leader. *"As-salamu alaykum! Oy ik? Mani egiwan? Mani echeghel?"* he said, without averting his eyes.

The priest translated the standard greeting, but found it strange that Aleck had greeted Kamara as a companion. That brute would never answer even the polite Arabic greeting with the standard response, *Wa-alaikumu s-salam*. But Aleck was buying himself some time.

Kamara smiled. He entertained himself with the Tuareg leader, but he was not afraid. He faced Aleck, taking off his glasses, and looked him up and down, answering in English, "Look here, you crazy man. Someone in your group has something that belongs to me. We traced the movement of the diamonds to Niamey, where someone tried to sell them. And the information we got was that he joined a large caravan. We are the RUF," he said, tapping his muscular arm on an ill-fitting tattoo of the initials of the Revolutionary United Front. "Some miners escaped from one of our mines after stealing our diamonds. Until we find out who they are, we are not leaving. Or do you want to see what we do with those who cheat us?" He puffed smoke in Aleck's direction.

The soldiers laughed and excitedly said they should kill one of the people as an example. As the priest translated for Aleck, the soldiers shouted, "RUF, RUF, RUF . . ."

Aleck looked steadily at Kamara, put his hands behind him, and moved even closer, lowering his head, almost touching his face to Kamara's. "There is nothing for you here. Take your soldiers and leave now. We don't want any trouble. We are selling our goods in the city. We don't have what you're looking for."

The situation became tense. The priest tried to soften Aleck's words as he translated. Kamara became enraged. He moved away from the Tuareg and ordered the boy soldier to shoot Abdar, who was in his sights.

CHAPTER 17

John wanted to know more. In fact, he would have loved to know it all at once. But the waiter politely informed them that the place was closing.

Before going home, Mádja said goodbye to John, but not without saying that the sequence of events would prove, by itself, that he was alive only by a miracle. And that for all that he had been through, he had no doubt of the extraordinary.

At home, he took a shower and went straight to his room. He lay down and admired his favorite print, depicting the arrival of Tuareg chief Moussa Ag Amastan in Paris in 1910. The veil, the sword, the pomp of a king, and his posture of authority.

Mádja never tired of imagining the scene portrayed there. Tuareg warriors are identified by the traditional sword, called *takoba*, and may also carry the *allagh*, or spear, and a shield called an *aghar*, usually only seen in ceremonies and celebrations or in ultratraditional confederations. Aleck evoked the warrior depicted in the painting, and his attributes had marked Mádja deeply. Not only that, but they had helped keep him alive.

Early the next morning, John and Mádja met again at Café de Flore. John, no longer needing the menu, greeted the waiter and quickly ordered two cappuccinos and two croissants *au beurre*, anticipating and fulfilling his friend's wish. They sat down facing the street while they commented on how spring was beginning to show its first signs. After a few sips of coffee and some small talk, Mádja picked up the story where he'd left off, precisely at the critical moment when his only friend was at gunpoint.

"John, you can't imagine the tension of that moment. Every second seemed to be the last of our lives. I cried, I trembled, I felt my body tense, and at the same time I could not move. Beside me, Abdar was begging for his life, while the tears streamed down, washing his face."

"These are situations that we think exist only in the movies. Surreal. I hope, my friend, that I can describe them adequately with words. You told me that Kamara ordered Abdar's execution, right?"

"Yes, and this would define our journey from then on," said Mádja, recalling the critical moment.

* * *

Aleck, even though he could not speak English, realized what was going to happen. He whistled loudly, and at the same instant more than fifty Tuareg rose up, surrounding the soldiers. They had been hiding, just waiting for a sign from their leader. They pointed their rifles at the militiamen, who had more modern weapons but were far fewer in number. Kamara hesitated. Furious about the ambush, he shook his head and suspended the execution. He gritted his teeth and looked around for a solution to the impasse.

The Tuareg chief looked at him once more and ordered them to surrender and drop their weapons. The priest translated his words, while Kamara decided his future. They were crazy, but not idiots. Under the sights of more than fifty rifles, they used what they had left of reason.

Weapons on the ground. The Tuareg surrendered Kamara and his soldiers, tying their hands and feet as one would tie pigs.

Under the priest's advice, the Tuareg put them on the backs of camels and a small entourage took them to a nearby town, where the local authority was to arrest them.

Defeated and humiliated, Kamara looked at Aleck, to memorize his face, swearing the Tuareg chief to death.

A relief was felt with the collective sigh. Abdar and I embraced and cried, sobbing, unable to say anything at that moment. We were coming back to life, with one more chance to walk. If he had been killed, I don't know what would have become of me. Abdar represented, at that moment, my only connection with sanity.

That same day, the Tuareg decided to move on, and the caravan got ready to leave. We were heading towards Mopti, flirting with the border of Burkina Faso and moving towards the famous Niger River. The *imageren* in front, stately and elegant as if nothing had happened. The *iklan* and Haratin, still frightened by the near tragedy, were walking even more quietly, trying to forget everything and move on. I couldn't take my eyes off Abdar. Still trembling, he did not even try to disguise the fright he had suffered. He moved in an automatic manner, his gaze on the infinite, as if still not understanding how he was alive.

CHAPTER 18

We walked almost the entire day, under a fine, refreshing rain. Abdar and I silently thanked the universe for life and the rain for hiding our tears. Stunned by what had happened, we ignored the exuberance of the fauna and flora along the way. Animals that I had never seen, and would have loved to meet, if the situation had been different. My father was passionate about animals. He knew all the species of Africa and lost track of time watching documentaries and reading *National Geographic* magazines. Pygmy hippos, small lizards with exotic features, and countless multicolored birds adorned our route. Green was still the backdrop of our journey through southern Mali, the last stretch of forest before the arid sprawl of the Sahara.

In the evening I finished my work and went out to look for Abdar. All day I wondered if he was the cause of the attack on our camp. After all, he had told me that he'd run away from a mining operation a few months before joining the caravan. When I found him, he was sitting next to Olaf, about to reveal the whole truth about the diamonds.

"Sit down, Mádja," said the priest. "Abdar will tell us why he risked everyone's lives this morning. And if he is really the person with the stolen diamonds," he added in a more serious tone, as he stepped aside so that I could sit down.

Abdar looked around, made sure no one could see us, and pulled out a bag with three small stones from his pocket. One of them was colored a pure, intense, vivid red, a very rare characteristic. Nobody knows for sure how a red diamond is formed. For its size and clarity, the stone could easily have fetched over a million dollars! The priest knew about the peculiarity of the stone. In fact, that man seemed to know everything. He knew the cupidity of diamond merchants and the frantic search for something of the sort.

"Do you think they will give up looking for these stones, Abdar?" he asked, as he tied the bag of diamonds and handed it back to Abdar. "You are risking the lives of all these innocent people because you stole them from a rebel-run mining operation, and you want to get rich? How did you imagine you could get away and be all right? What are you planning to do now?"

"Father, it is not at all what you think. I stole those stones, yes, but they don't know for sure what happened. They don't know how many stones were taken or who the miners are that escaped. If they were sure, they wouldn't have come here with only a few men. These stones alone are worth money that would justify bringing an army! First, I must explain to you what happens in Sierra Leone."

Abdar put the stones away and turned to face us.

"Since 1991, Foday Sankoh has controlled numerous mines throughout the country. He is an ex-military man who has been in prison and was a diamond smuggler. After being helped by Charles Taylor, who started the civil war in Liberia, and with the money he earns from diamonds, he has been raising an army. He founded the RUF, trains and buys weapons for this army, as well as cars, grenades, and even airplanes. He recruits uneducated, easily manipulated youth under the pretext of freeing them from the oppressive government. He blinds them, because in reality he only wants the money to buy more weapons and gain more power. They arrive in the villages, destroy everything, and set fire to the houses, burning the people alive. They kill the old people, rape the women, and kidnap the children to turn them into soldiers. They mutilate people..." Abdar swallowed hard and continued, "...who supported the government, saying that without hands or legs they won't be able to vote anymore. They coldly murder or indoctrinate kids. Some of these so-called soldiers are as young as seven years old! They make them get high, give them alcohol and force them to kill, including their own families, without remorse or pity. They create father figures in the gang and the boys become cruel and loyal to their bosses. There are many child soldiers in the country. The healthiest men are forced to work in the mines at gunpoint, day and night, defecating on the spot and eating the soldiers' leftovers. When there is something left! They exhaust them, so that they cannot escape."

Then I understood why my parents had fled Sierra Leone, and I felt even closer to Abdar, because we shared the sad coincidence of the civil war in that country.

"I was an English and French teacher in my village, Father," Abdar continued. "Before that, when I was a young boy, I had immigrated to Europe with an uncle on a clandestine boat. I went at my mother's request. She thought I would have a better chance this way. My uncle died during the trip, I don't even remember why. And I was on the streets of Genoa for a long time, I had to beg for food and even steal.

I ended up going from city to city until I got to Monaco, because I had heard that everyone there is rich. In fact, I never went hungry on the street, and someone always took me to a shelter, which looked more like a hotel. There, I got a job with a Belgian couple, the Courtoises, who practically adopted me and changed my story."

Abdar's eyes moistened.

"They were good to me in a world where I knew only evil. They were the light I needed. They taught me many things and made me understand the importance of education. I studied in Europe until I was twenty-three. But I couldn't stop thinking about my family, about my forgotten village. Until I came back to help my people. I always thought that everyone needs to study, that everyone deserves the opportunity to have knowledge. It was when I was in the village with my family, building a dream, teaching where no one has access to anything, that they came. I had time to take my mother and sister to a cave in the forest. I had to go back for my cousin Ismahil. When I arrived, I saw when they had placed his hand on the table." Abdar paused again, this time longer, took a breath and continued, "And he was asked, as they laughed, if he preferred long or short sleeves. This meant cutting his hand at either the wrist or the elbow. They seemed to be enjoying the situation. And Ismahil begged them not to do this to him, but they ignored him. When he didn't respond, they cut off both his hands and left him to bleed to death. I couldn't help myself. On an impulse, I ran to try to save him. That's when one of the kids saw me and shot. I was lucky."

Abdar pulled his shirt away from his left shoulder showing the scar resulting from the gunshot.

"The bullet hit me right here in the shoulder, exploding this bone that connects it to the trunk, so my arm is thinner, and my movements are limited. They took me away, saying that I was still good enough to work in the mines. I spent some months working as a slave, I don't know exactly how long." Abdar looked firmly at the priest. "Until the rebellion happened and I saw my chance to escape from that hell. It was my passport to escape from there. It was all or nothing. It was the opportunity to see my family again."

The priest's eyes expressed his pain at Abdar's suffering, as a tear trickled down his face.

"One night they brought women from a village they had attacked and had a party with lots of drugs and lots of drinking. This was normal in the camp, but that day they went overboard. We, the slaves, took advantage of that moment, got the guns, and shot anyone who moved. They were bullets filled with hate cooked up by injustice, by cruelty. We used all the strength we had left. I don't know if I killed anyone or not. But I did what I had to do to escape. As I was running away, I saw the purse of one of the soldiers on the floor. One of the diamonds had fallen out. It sparkled, even in the dim light. I didn't even think about it. I took the diamonds and fled into the mountains. Probably the other prisoners took some diamonds, too. I looked back and saw everything on fire and the slaves howling cries for freedom. I just wanted to get out of there. But I am pretty sure that they killed all the soldiers before escaping. I crossed the mountain. It was raining heavily! Almost in the morning, I saw my salvation pass by on the road in the form of humanitarian aid truck and I threw myself on the asphalt, begging them to help me."

Abdar paused and looked at the priest and me. Paralyzed, we tried to anticipate what happened next.

"They hid me among the supplies until they reached Conakry. There, an English reporter was moved by my story and convinced me to board a flight with a false identity. They were going to Niamey. There, Daniel, the reporter, could access data on refugees. There was no one with my mother's name or my sister's name in the database. He could not find out where my family was. I thanked him and said goodbye, and he told me to look for him in London as soon as I was out of danger. I decided to try my luck in Niger myself. I went to Niamey to try to trade the diamonds. After trying to sell them once or twice, I realized that it would be difficult to get a good price there, and because of the rarity of the red stones, I ran the risk of being robbed and seeing my dream come to an end. I knew I had to go to England and sell them there. That is when I heard about the Tuareg caravan from Assekrem and overheard two people talking that a peace agreement was being made between the Tuareg and the governments of Niger and Mali. Otherwise, the caravan would not have been able to pass through there. I also heard about the castes within the caravan. And when they mentioned the *iklan*, who are less noticed and work at the end of the caravan, I had the idea to join them and not be noticed. That way the story would have time to cool down, and I could make the crossing more safely, all the way to Tamanrasset."

"You did well, Abdar," said the priest in a calmer tone. "Trying to sell the diamonds would have been too risky."

"That's what I thought too, Father. Working and dressed in the right way, no one asked me any questions. I thank you, Father, because I know that you noticed me right away. Nothing goes unnoticed by you. You have always talked to me without questioning. And this is how I hope to get to Europe and sell these diamonds and then look for someone who has access to the refugees' data and try to find my family, wherever they are."

Abdar finished his story, emotional. With his hand over his eyes, he was trying to contain his crying. The priest stood up, kissed Abdar's head, and left without saying anything. I was crying, too, as I hugged my friend. Together, we further firmed our bonds of friendship, suffering the pains of Sierra Leone's cruel war over blood diamonds.

At first light of the next day, the caravan, unaware of our pain, set out on the road again. We looked at each other and words were no longer needed to express the bond that united us.

CHAPTER 19

"Henry, a double espresso and a chocolate roll, please," Mádja asked the now-familiar waiter. "And the same for my friend here."

"Chocolate bread? I confess that I don't usually eat chocolate at this hour. But when it comes to coffee and chocolate, two things I can't do without, you can't go wrong," said John, anticipating the taste of his first meal of the day.

"You will love it, my friend. The double espresso is to jog my memories. After that meeting with the RUF, we had a bit of a lull, as happens after storms," explained Mádja, resuming the narrative, between one bite and another.

* * *

Our caravan made its way towards the city of Mopti, doing small business in the smaller villages and towns along the way. Following a small river, which later would join the Niger, we traded our goods for corn, cotton, cereals, dates, and some small animals essential to daily life, such as goats. In the manner of those who walk without worrying what time is it, the Tuareg stayed, days and nights, wherever the commerce and the people welcomed them best. I never saw a Tuareg from that tribe asking the time. Their routine was a perfect dance with the rhythm of the earth's movement.

As we approached the cities, huge plantations cut across the forest for miles. The abundance of water, so scarce in the Sahara, kept delaying our return home. Abdar, Brother Olaf, and I cultivated a friendship that grew every day, cemented by mutual understanding about our origins, our stories, and our reasons.

I worked quietly, always attentive to the orders I received. My interest in the Tuareg grew with the courage and strength that they transmitted to me. They carried generations of warriors in their genes, countless battles in their blood, and feared no one.

As a reward for my good work and continued interest in helping, I was assigned to serve with one of the noblest families, a fact seen as an honor by the lower castes. This meant more prestige within the confederation, and better food. Nothing like a substantial meal after days of eating only goat cheese and mint tea and unsalted, coal-flavored bread.

I served a family that belonged to the Kel Rela, one of the most important tribes in the confederation. The Kel Rela had solidified their position within the Kel Ahaggar when Aleck married their most beautiful representative, Jlassi. The Kel Rela also had Kahina, who was about to marry to further strengthen the ties. Kahina and I were the same age. Inevitably, we exchanged glances and fed our youthful curiosity. The suitors who were chosen for her were much older and this was normal and expected. However, although traditional, the tribe had allowed Kahina to attend school, before they'd started again with the caravans. She'd developed a different worldview.

Women are essential in Tuareg society. They are responsible for preserving the Tamashek language, which has few written records. They pass down Tuareg culture through tales, poems, and proverbs from mother to child. The women, very graceful and always adorned with gold and silver, participate in the decisions of the tribe and accompany business trips like this one. They spend much of the day taking care of their appearance. They are also the ones who know how to play the *imzad*, like a violin, an exclusively female art. It is said that the desire to hear the music of this instrument again instills warriors with the courage and bravery needed against their enemies during battle.

Whenever I could, I tried to do my chores near Kahina's tent, fascinated by her exotic beauty and my forbidden love. Kahina had thin features, small dark eyes. Her skin captured a stunning array of dark tones. She wore a turban only on the top of her head, revealing the long braids that went halfway down her back. It was a sight that lifted my world to a place where there was no pain. It was momentary, like watching a great movie—as soon as it ends, you want to know more, see it again. I would finish my work and always ask if there was anything else I could do. Before being dismissed, I always left her a flower in her tent, strategically placed where only she could see. I wasn't sure if she approved of my gesture. But as long as I was not reprimanded, I took it as a good sign.

At the end of the day, as if the enchantment was over, I would return to my camp, where the nights were lulled by the sound of nocturnal animals and Tuareg legends. In the warmth of improvised fires, we cooked a meager but honest dinner. Conversations warmed by friendship, built in the mortar of suffering and daily coexistence. The moments of pain that insisted on visiting me in the solitude of the early morning attacked me with the poignant memory of my parents' death. My only consolation was listening to the priest's adventures, my friendship with Abdar, and the secret admiration and impossible love I had for Kahina.

In Abdar, the uncertainty of seeing his family reigned, mitigated by delusional dreams of wealth and power. He kept repeating his desire to become rich and find his family, while Olaf was increasingly afraid that his mission might suffer from the stubbornness of the Tuareg and the political instability of the region. The priest occasionally visited from the front of the caravan to tell us one of his many exciting but never-ending stories.

One such evening, Olaf sat down with us and told us a little more about this legendary Tuareg caravan, the larger purpose of our journey, and the magnitude of the terrain they had covered so far.

"The Tuareg people have suffered in recent years from an aggressive drought and violent separatist movements. Beginning in 1975, some young men got formal jobs, when the Algerian government decided to build hotels and schools in the Tamanrasset region. This was the reason why these young Tuareg abandoned their customs, such as nomadism, for example. In jobs like those, they earn their own money and therefore do not have to travel to exchange goods and merchandise as their people have always done. Some Tuareg children live at schools, where they learn French and Arabic, and naturally lose daily contact with their culture, with their roots. But the Kel Ahaggar, the group we are part of, need the success of this trip. They founded a cooperative to sell the goods of all tribes, years ago in Tamanrasset. That was an attempt to finally establish a united Tuareg community but for political reasons that has not been working. Add to this the drought and the recent conflicts. All this made Aleck decide that it was necessary to leave. He gathered the chiefs of the most traditional tribes and decided that they would trade their goods outside the desert. After this trip, they would return to Timbuktu, the land of his parents. There they would stay for a while to gather provisions and then return for good to Assekrem, the place where they belong."

"Father, were you with them in the desert too? I can't imagine how it is to walk in the desert," said Abdar, curious.

"Compared to the desert, we have here plenty of water and vegetation, and still I almost faint every day!"

"Oh yes, I participated in the whole thing and I can say that it was a superhuman effort! We left Assekrem towards In Guezzam and then to the salt reserves in Fachi. The Tuareg walk where no one else walks. They have owned these salt routes for a hundred of years. Nine million square meters of desert! I helped them make the ropes that tie the goods to the camels, on average twelve for each animal, and assisted with their negotiations for salt in Fachi. There, the only contact with the world is the caravans. If they end, the town will become isolated, perhaps forever."

"What about sandstorms?" I asked.

"Tell me about it! On the way out of Assekrem, in the first few days, I felt the force of the harmattan: the desert wind that sucks up all the moisture, disappears with the clouds, and lifts the surface layer of desert dust. The grains of sand become tiny daggers that dig into your face and force you to understand the reason for the turbans."

"This I want to see. So, even you have surrendered to the Tuareg turban," I said, smiling at the fact that we had never seen the priest turbaned in the camp.

"Yes, my friend. Not only to the turban, but to the customs that have kept them alive in the desert for all these years. At the beginning of the journey, we had some meat, but it had to be eaten quickly or it would have spoiled. The Tuareg women therefore prepared a paste of dates, goat cheese, corn, and flour from some root, which was the only food for several days or weeks of crossing the desert. When the heat was extreme, they dissolved the paste in a little water and drank it as a fortifier. The Tuareg and the desert respect each other. The crossing of the Ténéré, the 'desert in the desert,' the 'land of fear,' is something that every Tuareg has to go through. It is the nothingness within nothingness. I will never forget the bluish hue that covered us just before dawn and the orange yellow that foreshadowed the end of the day."

"And all this to get salt! I can't understand it. If the salt were diamonds . . ." commented Abdar, smiling.

"You and your diamonds!" I said, throwing a stone in Abdar's direction. "That's all that's going through your crazy head."

"Salt, kids, is extremely important in the desert and in the world. Aleck makes sure that only the best-quality salt is purchased. He dips a piece of grass in his saliva and stirs the salt to see if it turns orange. If it does, he buys it; if it stays the same color, he refuses. More than twenty-five thousand camels pass through Fachi every year!" said the priest, stretching his arms. "Ah, boys, all this is beautiful and fascinating, but now we must sleep. Tomorrow we start our walk again. It was good to be able to tell you a little more about the inexhaustible wealth of the Tuareg history."

"Twenty-five thousand camels? Wow! How many camels do we have in our caravan, Father?" asked Abdar.

"Ah, my friend. The Tuareg never talk about it. They fear the evil eye and think that if they count their camels, they will die," replied Olaf smiling, and then he said good night.

CHAPTER 20

The next day, in the heart of Mali, getting closer and closer to our final destination, Timbuktu. The villages moved us by their precariousness, displaying small mud houses with thatched roofs. They seemed to have been built without any tools, such was the architecture and the simple arrangement of the blocks. Each was one room, almost a tower, with a more or less square hole for ventilation and maybe also for rain. The beaten red earth, surrounded by interlaced sticks, delimited the area that must have belonged to a family. The so-called wall did not seem capable of containing the wrath of any animal that might want to invade it. We'd seen poverty all around, but we didn't know that it could be even worse. And this? This was the worst possible kind.

We saw only women entrusted with daily tasks, multicolored and adorned. Sad and impassive faces that hid a fascination for the strange, for the unknown. Perhaps they hid, who knows, the dream of seeing the world, of changing destiny, decided by the cruel determination to be born and die the same size. The routine imposed by the situation weighed on the sleepy eyes that we saw from afar.

We were continuing on our way, when a curious little girl approached, stunned at the sight of the Tuareg. Her head was adorned with a yellow cloth and silver earrings that sparkled in the sun. A floral dress with a blue background and flip-flops with pink details completed her outfit. She looked at the Tuareg with a blank expression, like that of te camels, saying nothing. The Tuareg pretended not to have seen any people and kept moving. Abdar, seeing something in the girl, slowed down and went towards her. Frightened, she at first turned away. He opened his bag and took out his favorite book. An old illustrated copy of *The Little Prince*, which he had read and reread, night after night, during the silent mornings we spent together. She smiled and thanked him. She ran back to her home and opened the book, looking as if she had won the world. Abdar caught up with me, happy with this unusual encounter.

"You gave your favorite book to someone who can't even read," I said, sneering at his gesture. "At least it has illustrations."

"Imagining is more important than reading. There is no change without imagination. Education is not a diploma, Footballer. Education begins with the possibility of thinking differently," Abdar added, smiling and shooting ahead, betting that he would reach the caravan before me.

I looked back and watched the girl, paralyzed, entranced by the book, until I lost sight of her and the small villages, forgotten in the unknowable interior of Africa.

I noticed a subtle change in the landscape. Ghostly branches appeared from nowhere and a long sequence of cut trees laid a brownish tinge on our surroundings. The Tuareg, however, seemed happy and more talkative than usual. The mood in the caravan had changed. The success of the negotiations had added up to the prelude to the final trek home.

There was the gigantic Mali ahead, but the trip did not overshadow their rituals. The routine was the road itself. In the midst of these events, they were preparing for a special occasion, one of the most important rituals of the Tuareg culture, which I had the pleasure of watching and experiencing up close.

CHAPTER 21

"John, more and more I discovered the richness of the tradition of this unique people," commented Mádja. "I learned to respect the differences and not to make judgments based only on my notions."

"I can hear your admiration when you talk about them, my friend," John replied.

The writer wrote down every detail, striving not to miss a single word. He benefited from the precise way his friend told his story and noted not only the facts of his narrative, but Mádja's impression of each moment.

* * *

I heard, in the distance, the sound of an instrument I didn't know and I was curious. On the farm, the Christian mission had taught us a little singing and keyboard. I confess that I had rather limited ability in both areas. I did, however, understand something about music, and the melody that spread through the camp was an absolute novelty to my ears.

It was the *imzaden*—the Tuareg violins with a single string—which played the melody while poems were sung. I approached and darted through the upper-caste camp, which I had been forbidden from entering this evening. I saw the priest, sitting farther away, watching from afar, and pulled on his habit, "Father, Father!"

"Mádja?" he said, startled. "What are you doing here? You know they don't want people from other castes on this side of the camp right now."

"Excuse me, Father. But I heard this song and I was curious. It is so beautiful!" I insisted. "What's going on?"

"Okay, let's sit in a spot where they won't see us and I'll explain."

We found a place where we could watch without being noticed and sat down. The priest asked about Abdar, and I told him that he was tired and had gone to bed early. I observed the appearance of Aleck, who seemed nervous, pacing in circles near his tent. I couldn't imagine what could make such an imposing and fearless warrior behave like that.

I admired, more and more, the freedom, the harmony with nature, and the strength of these traditions. Aleck, for me, was the greatest representative of these ideals, the main source from which I learned the qualities of these extraordinary people.

"Father, why is he so nervous?" I asked. "Shouldn't he be happy about this whole party?"

"It is hard for a man to be indifferent to the arrival of his first son . . . or daughter," he explained, smiling. "Aleck's wife, Jlassi, is about to give birth. The first son, or daughter, will come into the world, with the great challenge of keeping the tradition that the father values so much or of giving in to the modern and risking diluting the soul of his people in the process."

"Who are the elderly women around the tent?"

"Wait and see, my dear friend," answered the priest, reticent.

The sound of the first chords of the next song entering our ears was bad. However, it only took a few minutes for us to feel a slight sensation of trance, as if the notes were connecting with some part of our soul. From then on we vibrated to the same sound, making micromovements with our bodies, following the rhythm and the pulsing of the magical and hypnotizing melody. Delighting in the bucolic sound of the *imzaden*, Olaf and I watched the old women enter the tent.

I have no idea if the birth was made easier by the music or the environment it had created. I could, even though I had to pay extra attention, hear the screams and groans of pain common during childbirth. I had never attended a birth before and it was not something I'd intended to do so soon.

I believe an hour later, we saw one of the elderly women, perhaps the maternal grandmother, come out of the tent with the baby on her lap. She joined the others, who began to walk around the tent, singing, according to the priest's translation:

> The old woman is leaving
>
> Fatima and Aisha are coming in
>
> Shoo! Shoo! Fatima and Aisha will cut your
> hair in the morning

After several turns, the leader of the group buried a knife in the sand, ending the baptism ritual. With this action, they believed they would protect the mother and the baby from the Old Woman, a spirit of the forest, according to Tuareg belief. Fatima and Aisha are the names of the wife and daughter of the prophet Muhammad. The grandmother finally handed the baby over to Aleck, who, overcome with emotion, held it up and shouted to the whole tribe, "He is an *imageren*! And his name will be great among the Tamust! He will be called Mohamed ag Farka!"

Aleck then sacrificed a ram, cutting its throat in the direction of Mecca and saying prayers, as the Muslim custom dictates.

The priest was considered an *inselmen*, or a marabout. These are the ones who take care of religion and the application of the Koranic laws. In the case of the priest, who was Catholic, he was accepted because of the respect the Tuareg had for him his help to the people. The Tuareg do not practice religion strictly and mix some Muslim practices with other traditions. They pray to the deities of the desert, of water, stone, fire, and mountains. The rituals were a great mixture of religious and cultural traditions.

Aleck, in honor of his firstborn, began the celebrations. One of the elderly women cut a lock of the child's hair and gave it to his father, who kept it in an amulet. By placing the jewel on his chest, he would carry his son forever close to his heart.

"Tamust, Tamust!" repeated Aleck, excited.

The priest translated, explaining that Tamust was the name of the entire Tuareg nation. I smiled, delighted with the richness of these traditions. Even though I was not a Tuareg, I was beginning to feel a kinship.

The joyful atmosphere that had formed continued, but they stopped playing the *imzads*. Out of nowhere, as if rehearsed, four elders each brought a small drum and began beating them in rhythm. The elders walked away, and the atmosphere changed, creating suspense.

"Why did the violins stop, Father?" I asked, disappointed.

"The drum is more representative for them at this moment," said the priest. "This is the ritual of the *guedra*, which means 'drum' in Tamashek. This instrument is made of clay, covered with skin—as women were created, according to tradition. In this way they perform the customary dance to celebrate birth, friendship, and marriage."

They put out the side fires and left only the central one lit. A woman with a black veil came out of the larger tent. In the ritual, she represented darkness and chaos. Her hands swayed towards the four cardinal points, also representing the four elements: air, earth, fire, and water. With her body, she showed the order of the universe's creation. Each gesture had several meanings, which even the priest did not know. He had seen this dance only once before in the camp. It was rare that he did not know something.

They lit all the bonfires and countless torches, which drew parallel lines on the ground. The drums beat faster, until the dancer fainted in a trance. The drumming began again, and everyone sang and followed the music, shaking their heads with their eyes closed. The single men and women lined up facing each other. It was time for the *ahal*, the ceremony of love. Also rich in gestures and body language, the ceremony is an enigma to outsiders. As I watched, I discovered that the men drew a circle on the women's hands and pointed at them as in a declaration of love. The priest told me that in Tuareg culture, however, it is the woman who decides. If she takes the boy's right hand and with her forefinger draws a diagonal line back and forth, it means, 'Leave everything behind and come with me.' If she draws a line only forward, it means, 'Leave everything behind and don't come back.'"

My eyes were scanning the suitors, when my heart almost leapt out of my chest as soon as I realized that Kahina was also part of the dance. My feelings for her, even though forbidden, had grown over the past weeks. I continued to court her, in the illusion that she would one day reciprocate. And Kahina had begun to respond to the flowers I left as gifts with small gestures, such as little hand-carved wooden horses, that she made herself, in which she hid some snacks and special foods that only noblemen had access to. This was the definitive proof that she also nurtured something for me.

Yet, to my dismay, there she was. Ready to get married and walk away, once and for all, from our youthful love. I approached the dancers, not worrying about not being seen. It was my love, my first love. I thought it was love. I certainly felt that way. Olaf warned me, but I wanted a closer look. He put himself in front, we came closer, but this time we could be seen.

"You see, Mádja, aren't they special?" said the priest, moved.

"Huh? What?" I answered, not understanding.

My concern and focus were different than his.

"I asked if they are not special," repeated the priest, without taking his eyes off the ceremony.

"Oh yes, they are, Father. She is very special!" I added, then suddenly afraid I had said too much.

* * *

At that moment, Mádja was admiring Kahina and her family. Their relationship remembered him of his parents, whose tragic death he could not forget. The images flashed in his mind, day and night. No matter what he did, they kept coming back to haunt him. Without warning, the weight of his conscience descended upon him, crushing him. And this aggravated guilt gave way to extreme shame for the fact that he had been able to do nothing to help his parents. Guilt and shame added up to anger at a faceless enemy. Mádja had watched the attack, he knew who they were. The faces he remembered, however, were the faces of evil. No defined features, no explanation. Irrational, destructive. Dealing with the gratuitous evil of man hurts the soul in a way that is difficult to heal. Who knows, perhaps love, the greatest force in the universe, could heal the deepest wounds of his soul.

* * *

"Who are you referring to? Kahina? I forgot that you have been serving her family. She is the only one without a definite match, because her marriage is the most important among the tribes. She doesn't want to get married. She told me that she considers herself too young and wants to learn more before she gives herself to someone and starts a family. However, there is an alliance being built between the two largest tribes and she is the key part," he added, feeling sad for me. "I know the boy, he is shrewd. He keeps asking me about her and always mentions Dassine, the raisin of the desert, the most famous Tuareg poetess, the queen of love and the messenger of peace. I bet he will win her over."

"And I bet not," I replied hopefully.

The Tuareg boy approached and extended his hand to Kahina. She held his right hand, drew a line forward, saying. "What do these veils under which you hide matter? I push them aside like the sun moves away from the clouds," she teased, quoting Dassine.

The boy smiled confidently. He looked the girl in the eye and replied, "The water murmurs, and I love you when you touch my lips with the softest of kisses," quoting one of the most famous verses of the same poet.

Kahina looked deep into her suitor's eyes. She paused for a second, under everyone's tense gaze. I was breaking into a cold sweat. I stepped forward a little more, until the priest held me by the arm. I wanted her to see me and look into my eyes. The beating of the drums and my heart added to the suspense and were the only sounds I could hear. The union of the two tribes subjects respect for the traditions and the choice made by a girl. She carried the power to unite, or to postpone the agreement between the tribes of secular tradition. Static, Kahina looked at her family and, to my surprise, turned her gaze to me. The decision she would make next would define the future of the tribes and ours as well.

CHAPTER 22

In the camp, at the height of the ceremony, Kahina turned her gaze to her suitor and withdrew her hand, resuming her original place in line. She did not draw the line back on the boy's hand, to everyone's surprise and his as well. It was as if the whole tribe had sighed deeply and stood in shock. A second of absolute silence. I think even the drums fell silent. Walking backwards, she looked quickly in my direction, with a shy smile, multiplying my dreams to infinity. Smiling, I looked at the priest, silently gloating that I had known she would not give herself to him. It was impossible to contain my joy. Olaf looked at me, shaking his head, and said, "Huh! Interesting!" He then got up and went to sleep, while I watched Kahina explain to her family what to them would be inexplicable.

By tradition, however, it was her right to have the last word.

CHAPTER 23

Early in the morning, John arrived with his friend at Les Deux Magots. Taking advantage of the balmy weather with no wind and the sky the most beautiful shade of blue possible for the season, they chose a small table outside.

"A *café crème et* one *gâteau au chocolat* for me, please," John asked, as usual mixing English and French.

"A green tea and a fruit tart for me, please," said Mádja in lightly accented French. "We have entered the final half of my journey with the Tuareg. How many things I have relived! I hope I haven't hurt the story with my emotions. It's hard to recount without reliving everything," sighed Mádja, settling down in the small chair.

"Don't worry, it's been a great experience listening to you," John said, opening his notebook. "You make my job easier because of the way you narrate. A story without emotion is just another story. But yours goes beyond that."

"Right. Let's go to Mali, the great and wonderful Mali," said Mádja, while the waiter served them. "There, once again, we experienced situations that I have only seen again since in Hollywood movies."

"One second, Mádja," John said, turning on the tape recorder.

* * *

In Mali, the caravan approached the city of Mopti and also the legendary Niger River. Olaf asked the Tuareg chief if Abdar could serve him. In this way, the three of us would be close to the nobles, since I served my dear Kahina's family and could accompany him at the front of the caravan. The priest usually refused servants, but he used the request as a pretext to have us always at his side, as he had taken a liking to us. Since he always walked, despite the chief's insistence he ride a camel, Olaf continued, step by step, with me and Abdar. We could talk and have some extra time to get to know each other better.

Olaf delighted in books about Africa. Before he left Europe for the first time, he'd studied the history of the African continent in depth and had been enchanted by the mysteries of Mali. He knew, in detail, what was known to few. And he enriched our sometimes tedious trip with stories of a past empire that had existed there. He told us that Mali had been very powerful. That in the thirteenth century, Sundiata Keita controlled business in the Sahara and several gold mines that spread as far as Senegal. One of his successors, King Abubakari II, sent an expedition to the unknown seas. Of this expedition, only one ship returned. This boat told stories of huge rivers flowing into the ocean. Imagine, discovering America two centuries before Columbus. At that time, large cities developed as centers of culture, financed by the abundant riches. Especially Timbuktu, which, "God willing, we will get to know," said the priest.

Since I didn't know anything about anything, I thought the country was still rich. The priest explained, though, that the empire had been extinguished and that the country was now miserable and more than half of the population lived in poverty. Unfortunately, a very common story throughout Africa. Due to the misery, colonization, drought, and civil wars, the Tuareg of Mali took refuge in Libya. Only a few years before had they started to return to northern Mali. The important thing was that the reinsertion of the Tuareg would be sensitive, generating great social and cultural differences and making our crossing riskier.

The Malians in the south had vehemently contested the peace agreement. In the north, criminality and mistrust reigned. And the liberation groups were fighting internally, causing divisions to form, including some quite violent and fundamentalist small groups. And we walked there, towards danger, I saw the possibilities of getting justice for what had happened to my parents fading away. Far from the place where the tragedy happened, with no resources and no one who could help me, what could I do? Resign myself to the idea that the murderers would never be judged? Accept the fact that my parents had died for nothing? After all, violence and cruelty were not unique to the region where I lived. I thought about surrendering to the Tuareg for good and living this new life, forgetting everything I'd had until a few weeks ago. I could accept servitude to avoid the fear of being by myself and having to make decisions.

The priest was talking, as usual. He didn't even stop to breathe. And I thought about all this, alternating between curiosity and reflection. Olaf went on to say that there had been several coup attempts in the country. And now some

Tuareg, trained by Gaddhafi, had formed real militias. They wanted to reclaim their territory. "Mali will have to manage this great ethnic conflict in the north," he added, showing concern. "And if no peace agreement is reached, this could cause us big problems during our crossing of the country."

The conversation with the priest left both Abdar and me frightened. We shared a past of tragedy and early suffering. He just wanted to get to Europe and find his family. I, even though I had no definite goal, at that moment only wanted peace. Every image of violence triggered the worst memories in my mind. Not only of the murder of my parents, but of our near death in the camp.

"Why don't you tell all this about the fighting to the boss?" Abdar asked Olaf in a harsh tone.

"My son, how many times have I tried to convince him to go back the way we came? But he doesn't think like us. As I said before, he wants to stop in Timbuktu, the city of his ancestors." He shrugged his shoulders. "He admits no other way but through what he calls 'the door to the desert.'"

Confirmation of the priest's fears was on the way. Some residents of the villages around the city of Mopti received us with suspicion. There was still the terror of the massacres of the civil war, which, although weakened, was not officially over. Although we could not avoid crossing through Mali, the priest at least sang victory by getting the caravan to avoid going through the capital, Bamako.

The climate and vegetation had changed. Africa browns hand in hand with green, thanks to the proximity of the Niger River. Plantations that took advantage of an archaic but effective irrigation system took turns with long, stony grasslands. Crossing a small river, the rocks took over the landscape and blended in with the few trees.

On the outskirts of Mopti, we stopped, once again looking for an old trading partner. In the camp, Abdar and I were living the Tuareg culture. The immersion, the day-to-day life, the closeness, and the repetition of tasks were beginning to leave their deep mark on us. We observed and commented on how happy the Turaeg were to be together. How the children ran free and learned to listen to the sounds of nature. They sharpened their senses, were trained to be guided by the sun and the stars, despite increasingly accessible modern tools. Young people my age wanted to ride the camels and be guided by them to where there was water. The adults were joyful and spontaneous, using everything they could find, always remembering the desert, where everything is scarce and everything has an enormous value. They seemed to live only in the present, the only moment in which life happens.

"I am sad to be happy," I told Abdar, as we prepared the shipments of handicrafts.

"What's up, Footballer?" asked Abdar, not understanding.

"I don't think I have the right to be happy after what happened to my parents," I said, swallowing my tears. "And I feel happy, being with the Tuareg, with you and the priest as friends, and with Kahina near me. It's not fair, it's not right!"

"My friend, what happened, happened. You can't change the past. Which doesn't mean that you have to forget it," Abdar said, as he put his good arm around my neck. "Give the past the homage it deserves, and look at your life as a present. You are alive by a miracle. It is a mystery. You owe a debt to the dead to do the best you can. Sad for what happened, yes, but happy for life and opportunity, for sure. Hopeful for love. Ah, boy, love makes all things new," he said, making me smile and see everything from a different angle, as he had a gift for doing.

CHAPTER 24

Hadj was the personal servant of our chief, Aleck. We were chatting, helping the women sort the material for the crafts when he appeared and told the priest that the chief was demanding his presence. According to him, Olaf would form, with Aleck and his wife, a small committee that would go to the city to do business. The priest asked that Abdar and I accompany him, knowing that we would enjoy making the short trip, seeing the movement of a real town after so many weeks on the road with only the animals and the sporadic small villages we'd seen along the way. Olaf had emphasized to us that he considered us friends disguised as servants. He wanted us to understand this point. Hadj promptly packed and saddled an animal for each one of us in the entourage at the request of his commander. Aleck did not want to linger in the city, and to save time, he'd ordered that no one should go on foot.

Hadj was a very interesting figure. Almost a comic book character. Son of a former slave and a Tuareg. Tall, dark, and exaggeratedly thin. He carried, on his dry face, the mark of privation. He wore a short white turban of bad cloth and wide blue pants tied with a rope. He only ate dates and pieces of unleavened bread with goat cheese; he drank tea, water, and rarely milk. He always worked with Aleck and took care of whatever the boss needed, without ever complaining. In the camp, everyone swore that he only answered his master's questions. Abdar and I had a bet going on who could make Hadj say at least one word. Whoever succeeded would win an extra slice of cheese from the other's portion. Until that moment, we were tied, because neither of us had had the courage to face him.

Hadj believed he owed his life to the Tuareg chief. As a teenager, he lived in an *inofok*, a community of people descended from former Tuareg slaves, near In Guezzam in southern Algeria. One day, after digging a well all morning, he stopped to rest, leaning back against one of the large black boulders that stand in that part of the desert. He was bitten by a yellow viper with brown spots. Overworked and underfed, he quickly felt the effects of the poison. It was then, by a miracle, or by fate, according to Hadj himself, that the young Tuareg warrior appeared, and with one clean shot, killed the animal. Still a boy, Aleck took Hadj to a lady in In

Guezzam who cured him with a remedy made from the tail of a desert lizard called *dolb*. Cured, Hadj sought out Aleck and vowed to serve him and his family for the rest of his life. Even though Aleck insisted on releasing him from the debt, Hadj refused. Aleck had saved him twice. First from the poison, then from the snake. The desert people believe that if you do not kill a viper that has attacked you, it will pursue you forever.

Ready and assembled, we went with our small entourage into town, in search of a local merchant named Mustapha, but known as the Geezer. He was a Mozabite, also a Berber, like the Tuareg. Mozabites lived in the vicinity of several oases scattered across the northern Sahara. The Geezer's parents had immigrated to southern Mali, fleeing the various rebellions that had ravaged the Sahara. They were well known among the Tuareg and the Geezer was a mandatory stop for anyone doing business in the region.

On the way to the warehouse, we stopped by a village famous for its good water, for its abundant well. We wanted to water the animals and fill the canteens. Aleck took advantage of the small local market to give Jlassi a present. Traveling with her, I couldn't help but admire the way she behaved and dressed. Jlassi had sun-browned skin, a beautiful color that highlighted her greenish eyes, which could only be appreciated on bright days. They seemed to borrow the brightness of the sun, and her sharp gaze seemed to land only on her husband. It was impossible to stare into her eyes for more than a few seconds. She wore a golden veil, fastened on both sides with a kind of crosspiece encrusted with colored stones, the largest of which, red, stood out in the center. It would be difficult to use any other word but majestic to describe her. Formally, she was not a queen, but certainly, in her bearing, actions, and spirit, she could be considered so.

I saw when Aleck bought her a necklace, perhaps the only adornment she lacked. He put it around Jlassi's neck, showing how much he respected her by the care and kindness of his gesture. But I found the peculiar pendant strange. It was a beautiful and unique symbol. It was composed of four identical circles arranged in a square. In the middle, a small hollow space in the shape of infinity. He said she should wear it for her protection. Jlassi had just finished her postpartum recovery, and the short trip and the gift certainly must have made her feel special and valued.

Next to the market in the village, a group was beginning a musical performance. The priest, recognizing them immediately, explained that they were the *griots*, considered to be the memory of the country. They played the *kora*, a twenty-one-stringed type of lute resembling a banjo. Olaf finished by saying that Mali is home to incredible musicians, including famous names such as Salif Keita, "the Golden Voice of Africa." With our canteens and hearts full, our animals satisfied, we resumed our journey towards our destination.

CHAPTER 25

We arrived in town and headed for a warehouse at the end of a pier. There was almost no movement of boats or people along the pier, except for a small craft fair. The building was quite large, almost square. It was dirty on the outside and clearly had not recently been painted or renovated. The wooden windows were large and looked as if they were about to fall in. Next to the staircase of twenty short steps leading inside was an archaic structure for tethering the camels or horses of those who came to do business there.

Aleck and Jlassi dismounted, directing us to tie up the camels. Once this was done, he called the priest to accompany him. Olaf motioned for Abdar and me to accompany them. Aleck would not need the priest's translation in this particular negotiation, but he trusted that Olaf could help him obtain the greatest benefit for the Tuareg. Jlassi, who would not be participating in the negotiation, crossed the street and stood looking at the small stores in the marketplace, comparing them to the handicrafts that she and other Tuareg were creating. The Geezer was waiting for Aleck at the top of the stairs to the warehouse.

He seemed to find the Tuareg's unlikely entourage strange: a serious-looking guy dressed in a terrible-quality cloth, a short white man in strange brown robes, and two scared young boys with their eyes roaming all over. The Geezer was short and fat, with hair halfway down his rounded head and floppy ears. He wore a full mustache on top of a black beard, speckled with gray hairs. Deep furrows marked his face, giving it a tired and excessively aged appearance, which probably gave him his nickname. He dressed his own way, differently from the customs of the region and of his native people. He invented wearing a white coat with blue details, which he never took off, and wide blue pants of the same color as his clothes.

* * *

The Geezer always carried a pen and a pad of paper, on which he did the calculations for his negotiations by hand. The calculations were made in front of the customer and the verdict was given on the spot. He greeted Aleck and the priest, paying no attention to Hadj, Abdar, and Mádja, as they were mere servants. He invited the group into the warehouse, looking down the street to make sure no one was passing by. He closed the main door. He gave the excuse that in special negotiations he preferred privacy. He didn't want any distractions. The large, heavy wooden door required a huge effort, and he could barely close it. He locked it so that it would not be opened from the outside. Aleck frowned and looked around, finding this attitude strange and sensing that something was wrong. Mustapha was overly friendly, talking too much. He reminisced that he had traded with Aleck's parents. Normally, he did not behave like this. Aleck remembered previous negotiations, when the Geezer had spoken coldly, disdainfully. He'd behaved as if he were doing the Tuareg a favor by buying their products. Maybe he had changed.

* * *

Locked inside, I saw when one of the employees entered through a narrow side door, all rusted out. The noise of the door closing caught everyone's attention. Another employee opened a larger door in the back and left it ajar. I remember the priest telling me later that he'd realized that they were armed when we first entered. I hadn't seen anything until that moment. When everyone entered the warehouse, there was a great silence. That millisecond, the absolutely deafening instant that precedes disasters. In those moments, it is as if time itself is suspended, waiting for what comes next.

CHAPTER 26

John was not aware of his sleep or the time. Mádja did not work on that day and they'd taken advantage of it to get ahead with the story. They'd enjoyed the day, had had lunch and dinner together. And it was already past two in the morning. But the story narrated by his friend left him lit up and curious. At some moments, Mádja paused, as if he wanted to narrate more slowly. Maybe it was the weight of reliving so much tension. Or perhaps it was the maturity of someone who now knows the danger and is no longer fooled by adolescent omnipotence.

The next day, a Sunday, Mádja was taking a large group on a city tour and could not meet John. They agreed to resume as usual on Monday, at the usual café, at eight in the morning.

John took advantage of his day off to take a quick stroll. He visited the Paris Book Fair at Porte de Versailles, which that year honored Japan, diverting his attention from Mádja's story for a while. He ate lunch alone, after hearing the news from home that Lilly and the baby were fine. In the evening he reviewed his notes and catalogued the recordings so far in chronological order. He did his best to go to bed early to make sure he would get a few good hours of sleep before hearing the final chapters of the book.

CHAPTER 27

John woke up very early that Monday. He left the hotel and walked to the appointed place. He saw some cafés and stores opening, in the mechanical preparation of those who receive hundreds of customers a day. They turned off the alarm, swept the floor, collected the garbage, checked the stock, and prepared the food. Again and again. John sat in the café, one of the first to open. And from there he watched everything, not thinking of anything specific.

He slowly took up the story again, rereading his notes from the week. The moment demanded much of his skill as a writer. He would have to balance the cold writing, the black and white, with the complexity of the emotions that would follow. He was excited, but also worried. But he had the feeling he would know how to do it.

Mádja arrived a few minutes late. He asked forgiveness and blamed himself for oversleeping. He ordered a sparkling water and a triple espresso. And soon it was back to the moment when they were locked in the Geezer's warehouse, surrounded by armed men.

* * *

In a dark corner of the warehouse, we saw a figure. He entered through the back door and emerged puffing a thick cigar. Clapping his hands and smiling, Kamara revealed himself under the light and pointed a pistol at Aleck. He nodded to the henchman who'd come in behind him to close the door. Aleck, by reflex, reached for the sheath of his sword, but could not find it. He'd left it on his camel. Hadj, his servant, made a motion to draw his weapon. The henchman at the side door who'd passed himself off as a warehouse employee made a negative sign to Aleck and the servant. Sarcastically, he smiled, asking for their weapons and taking them with ease.

We remained static. I couldn't believe what I was seeing, and I felt my body tense up. I was panting, sweating, my mind racing, reliving the tragedy of my parents and the assault on the camp. And there he was, the head of the militia, unmistakable, with his left ear cut off and the same evil expression. A psychopath taking delight in having people under his control, to crush them at any moment like cockroaches. I had anger, hatred, but all of it was clouded by fear, dread, and the feeling that I couldn't go through this again.

We watched, paralyzed, foreseeing a tragic outcome. Kamara took another drag on the cigar, holding it in his teeth. He slowly let out the smoke, like the master of the situation. From his pocket he took out a black bag, which, from the noise, was full of stones. He looked at the Geezer and threw it at his chest.

* * *

"Diamonds buy everything. They buy guns and cars, make wars, and why not, destroy old friendships. Every man has his price!" he said, smiling, while the Geezer counted his profit.

Aleck looked with disgust and surprise at the Geezer. The Geezer had betrayed not only the Tuareg chief, but an entire nation, Aleck's ancestors, his parents and grandparents. The Geezer became an object of contempt for Aleck, and Aleck did not remain silent about the situation. It was not necessary to understand the language to understand Aleck's indignation at this unfaithful trap.

"Where have the years of trade between our peoples gone? Where is the memory of your father, an honorable man and friend of the Tuareg nation? Where is the trust we placed in you? Are these stones worth your character? Are they worth the breaking of a word given from generation to generation? Are they worth the loneliness that now awaits you?"

The Geezer counted the stones and saw that Kamara had kept his word. He put them away carefully and looked at his former business partner and now enemy.

"My dear Aleck . . . I didn't want to lose such good business partners. But you Tuareg never tire of fighting. You claim your territory and then you call yourselves free peoples, the 'wolves of the desert'! Why can't you be content with the reservations that the government has proposed? No! You need to fight for a 'Tuareg nation.' And then you fight among yourselves as if the war with the government is not enough. Do you know how many Tuareg have traded with me in the last few years? None! Because they don't plant anymore, they don't have any more cattle, no more dates. They just want to go along with Gaddhafi and fight for an identity. Baloney!" He smiled sarcastically. "Times are tough, my friend, and business is business."

Kamara, who understood betrayal like no other, decided to add some spice to the situation. "And your little friend here has earned an extra stone for convincing the local militia that your gang is a branch of the rebels from the north. By now they should be celebrating in your camp with your family," he said, smiling. "Oh, I forgot that the crazy guy doesn't speak my language. Translate what I said to him! Every word of what I said," he added, speaking to the Geezer. "I want to see him suffer until the moment I decide he must die!"

The Geezer seemed to feel bad for the first time. There was still a spark of scruples, which suddenly made him waver. Stroking the diamonds in his pocket, he turned to Aleck and translated Kamara's words. He motioned to leave, but Kamara stopped him. He reminded him that the payment included taking the prisoners aboard his van, which he himself, the Geezer, would drive. That way, they could leave without being noticed. And he ordered the Geezer to get the keys, because they would be leaving soon. The plan was to take them as prisoners to a remote house on the outskirts of Douentza. There, Kamara had set up his headquarters, waiting for the right moment for revenge. He would torture them without haste. He wanted to make sure they knew nothing about the stolen diamonds in Sierra Leone. Besides, Kamara would take pleasure in seeing the Tuareg suffer and make an example of what happened to those who stood up to the RUF. It was a matter of honor to take revenge on the Tuareg chief and show strength before his commanders.

Aleck acknowledged the blow. His expression changed, his dark skin, bluish from the veil, lost some depth. The thought of his only son being killed by cowards clearly consumed him. I could see that every muscle in his long, slender arms was ready for all or nothing. He looked at Hadj, his servant, in the sights of another guard. They knew each other like few people know each other. Hadj made an affirmative sign with his eyelids.

* * *

Sensing the meaning of the servant's sign, I held Abdar's wrist. The priest, also sensing the action, thought of saying something to Aleck, but had no time.

With the adrenaline of the moment, Aleck revealed all his Tuareg rage. Skillfully, he drew a dagger from inside a false pocket, launching it at Kamara's left shoulder. The dagger landed in an exact spot between the mercenary's shoulder and chest, tearing the pectoral muscle, which made him drop his weapon immediately. Aleck's movement, however, did not prevent Kamara from firing a shot in his direction, hitting his left flank. As he threw the dagger, Aleck's elbow hit the priest's face, causing him to fall, unconscious. The action also caused the Geezer, frightened, to try to run away. At the same time, Hadj jumped onto one of Kamara's guards and suffered the impact of another shot. Fallen, the two began to fight over the gun.

Abdar and I were acting out of reflex or survival instinct, call it what you will. We advanced towards the Geezer, who wanted to open the main door so he could escape. Kamara was trying to pull the dagger from his shoulder. He tried to reach for the pistol with his other hand, however it was close to Aleck, who took it up and shot him, missing by centimeters. Scared, the henchman next to Kamara helped the boss to his feet, shooting back without aiming. They both escaped through the back door, towards the jeep. At the front door, the Geezer found himself with no way out. He pulled out a short curved knife with a gold-plated bone handle and pointed it in our direction. Aleck saw Kamara running away and could do nothing due to the shot to his abdomen. So he turned his attention to us, who were at the point of the Geezer's curved knife.

The Geezer tried to bargain his escape with us. He was the kind of guy who would rather negotiate than fight, because, as it turned out, he had never won a fight in his entire life.

"A stone for each of you to let me go," he said. "I leave and you win, and I don't have to stab anyone," he added, smiling, as if it were the best possible offer.

Aleck picked up Kamara's gun from the ground. He wielded it and closed his left eye. He aimed very quickly and fired a shot into the Geezer's heart, silencing him forever. The Geezer brought his hand to his chest under the impact of the bullet and his legs failed him. He fell to his knees, looking at Aleck, as if seeing that the outcome had been well deserved. The whizzing sound of the bullet that killed the Geezer shocked everyone. Aleck dropped the gun on the floor and motioned for Abdar and me to attend to the priest, while he sat down in a chair before passing out. There was no time to assess what had happened. One reaction led to another. Abdar woke the priest with a few slaps on the face, while I opened the door and saw a scene that should have been nothing new to me.

CHAPTER 28

Mádja looked out into the street, sighing like someone who needs fresh air. He turned to John and, after a short pause, said, "John, no matter how many times we witness such a scene, we never get used to it, at least not if we are normal people and are sober. This hurts a fundamental law that shouldn't even need to be written down, I think. That law is in our DNA: 'Thou shalt not kill!'"

* * *

In the fight with Hadj, the second henchman had managed to open the door, bringing the fight to the outside of the warehouse. Using what strength he had left, Hadj mounted the henchman's belly and squeezed his neck, slowly strangling him. He fell beside the body and felt the severity of his injury. Jlassi, who'd heard the commotion and the gunshots, ran towards the warehouse, thinking that something had happened to Aleck. As she approached, she saw Hadj on the ground, in agony, covered in blood. She told the servant that he would be fine and that Aleck would help him. Jlassi lifted Hadj's shirt and realized that his wound was extensive. There was a pool of blood on the floor.

Hadj looked at her and with difficulty, said, "I have fulfilled my destiny . . . I have paid my debt . . . I go in peace! Please tell this to my master."

"You are not going to die," replied Jlassi, moved. "I will do everything to save you."

She wanted to believe in the impossible.

"No! Let me go. Now I am really free. I will die in peace," he answered with his last strength. "I only hope that I have served your family as I should."

"You have served us best and most dedicatedly of all, my friend! You will always be with us, wherever we are. Go in peace, I will honor your memory," Jlassi finished.

She looked at him one last time and his peaceful expression comforted her.

Mádja watched it all from the warehouse door. His head ached, his breath quickened, and his legs buckled. He knew the feeling of dread that had been gripping him since what had happened to his parents. In the momentary silence of pain and crying, he heard the sound of a speeding car coming from behind the building. Kamara and his faithful squire were escaping with the gang's jeep. On their escape they saw the opportunity to still have some advantage over Aleck.

* * *

The henchman who was driving the car stopped with a hard brake. He'd seen Jlassi standing beside Hadj's body and assumed she was with the Tuareg, and he ordered her to get into the vehicle. Undaunted, she told him she would not go and looked at me for help.

The thug recognized me and shot me. The bullet grazed my right leg. He said that if she didn't get in the jeep, the next shot would be fatal. I didn't move. I was once again overcome with fear. I was shaking and crying. I lost control of myself. Jlassi gave in and climbed into the vehicle without saying anything. Kamara was in a lot of pain, yet he gave the goon the signal to speed up and shouted, looking at me, "Tell the Tuareg I will kill him!"

And they left, taking Jlassi as prisoner.

There wasn't time for much explanation. I was in shock, but I had no one to help me. I had to gather strength from where I thought I didn't have it. I went back to the warehouse and saw Olaf waking up. He looked around and realized the gravity of what had happened. Aleck was trying to get up, despite his injury.

Abdar saw the bag of diamonds beside the Geezer. He bent down and took it, knowing that he would need them. The priest saw Abdar take the diamonds and scolded him, sternly, "Isn't it enough pain that diamonds have already caused, Abdar?"

"Father, you know my motives. And what will these stones on the ground be used for? I will use them to help undo all that I have caused. I am sorry. None of this was supposed to happen," he said, putting the diamonds in his pocket.

"Father, we don't have time for this," I said. "They took Jlassi."

"Jlassi!" exclaimed Aleck, hearing his wife's name.

"It's not possible!" said the priest, shaking his head.

He translated what I'd said to Aleck, who became angry.

He shouted, "No, no, not my wife!"

We helped Aleck up, despite his initial refusal of assistance. We left the warehouse and saw that the camels were no longer there. They must have let them loose or taken them away before they came in and surprised us. I reminded the priest that the bandits had planned to escape in a larger car and that the vehicle could only be on the other side of the warehouse. Don't ask me how I remembered anything. I was still acting in an automatic way.

* * *

Aleck winced at his injury but told the priest that they needed to go back to the camp to see if his son and the others were okay, and then they would have to plan how to rescue Jlassi. He thought of the beautiful wife he loved so much as a hostage of those brutes. His newborn son might be killed if there was a surprise attack. The pain was too great. He looked to his right and saw Hadj's body lying, bloodied, on the ground. In a short time, he would have lost his servant and confidant, his beloved wife, and his only son.

He fell to his knees and wept copiously, defeated by hopelessness.

Abdar felt devastated. He felt guilty about it all, although deep down he knew there wasn't much choice.

The priest took Abdar aside and said, "I need you to do something for me: pay someone to bury Hadj in a dignified manner, and find out in which direction the jeep went," he said in a firm voice. "Use the stones you collected."

"Yes, Father. I will."

While I was returning to the warehouse and looking for the van keys, Abdar discovered a man to bury Hadj's body who told him that the jeep had left for Douentza. Abdar used one of the Geezer's stones and arranged everything as Olaf had requested.

* * *

The priest informed Aleck that Hadj would be buried with dignity. He also said that the camels had been taken away and that they needed to continue by car. As bad as the situation was, they still did not know the condition of the rest of the Tuareg caravan. I brought the vehicle around, but I barely knew how to drive. My father had taught me the principles with a farm truck, but I'd had no practice. Aleck, besides being wounded, had never driven in his life. The priest asked Abdar if he knew how to drive, and Abdar took the wheel, steering with his one arm.

Even with Abdar speeding through the streets, we returned to camp slower than we would have liked. In less than an hour, we spotted a few tents. Tension took over when we saw the smoke rising in the distance, giving us the impression that a cruel and intense combat had also taken place there.

CHAPTER 29

It was dawn in Paris. An uncomfortable drizzle was falling over the city. John woke up to a text message from Mádja asking him to come to his house. They would continue the story there. That day, some tourists had canceled their tours and Mádja had the day off. Without work, he would no longer go, as usual, to the center of Paris.

John rented a car from the hotel. He drove off shortly after receiving the message from Mádja. He arrived at the agreed time and parked in space seven, as his friend had told him. From his apartment window, Mádja waved and buzzed John in, opening the gate to the building. He waited for John at the door and thanked him for his willingness to meet him there. He pointed to the table next to the kitchen and invited him to sit down.

John admired the tasteful decoration. He was very complimentary, which pleased Mádja. There was a modern kitchen, with all the utensils of French haute cuisine. However, the appliance that caught his attention the most was the espresso machine. Mádja himself was truly enraptured by this ultra-modern piece of equipment, the center of his kitchen. And he explained to John the details of the contraption, as a proud father describes his son's qualities.

"You see, my friend, this little Italian beauty has a retro design, but it's modern! It is designed for those who, like me, want to extract the maximum flavor from their coffee. On the machine, I can trigger a timer to determine the time in which the coffee should be processed. In addition, it has a temperature display, allowing four settings for different types of beans and roasts. And for those, like you, who like to spoil their coffee by adding milk, I can steam it at the same time as I prepare the coffee," said Mádja, jokingly.

"Ha! Ha! Ha! It sounds like you are really in love with that machine. And, yes, I like lattes, but, thanks to you now, I prefer an espresso. You can send me the best that coffee machine has to offer," John replied, joining in the fun.

"John, I will prepare you a double espresso then."

"Excellent. Nothing better to wake me up for good to pick up where we left off," he said, opening his laptop and putting his tape recorder on the table.

While waiting for coffee and going over what his friend had told him the day before, he reflected on the richness of the hidden stories that each of us carries in our souls. The victories, the defeats, the mistakes, the hits, and the twists and turns. The coincidences and circumstances. Luck and fate. In short, each life is a complete book, with aspects of the human mystery fully intertwined.

"Let's pick up from the moment we arrived at the camp, shall we?" said Mádja, changing the tone of the conversation and preparing to start the narrative again.

"Yes, I am ready. What a situation, my friend! I try to stay impartial, focused on the text, but I am really sorry for all that you witnessed at such a young age."

"I understand. Like I said, I only believe it because it's my story. It was bad there. And it would get even worse!"

* * *

Back at the Tuareg camp, Aleck quickly got down from the van and went out looking for his son. He walked to his tent. The priest called Abdar and me and went through the fallen bodies, hoping to find someone still alive. Aleck found no one in his tent. The dead were scattered all over the ground. Tuareg and militia members. We were expecting the worst, when a small group of Tuareg who had survived the confrontation came out of the forest. They approached Aleck and told him how they had been surprised.

"Chief, they came in shooting. We had very little time to react. We managed to save the women and children, including your son. What should we do now, sir?" asked the warrior.

"Take me to my son," he replied, relieved.

Aleck took a deep breath and continued ordering as they walked, "Then collect the necessary weapons and supplies. Choose the fastest camels and don't carry extra weight. Two of you will follow with the survivors and my son along the secret Niger road. The other three will come with me by car. They have taken Jlassi. We must rescue her. We are going after the kidnappers to put an end to this story. We will meet in Timbuktu when this is over. Look for my parents' house on the east side of town and wait for my signal. My brother still lives there and everyone knows him. Ask for Mohamed ag Bakri. He will protect you. If I don't show up in three days, go to Assekrem and wait for news."

Aleck was showing signs that his wound was bothering him. He tried at all costs to hide the bloodstain under his clothes. He gathered his strength and went to meet his son. When he saw Mohamed, he took the baby in his arms. Aleck placed his forehead against Mohamed's and closed his eyes. He said some words, looking up to the sky as if he was thanking Allah that his son was alive.

I broke all propriety and ran to Kahina. She was the only one in her family who had escaped the massacre. She was still in shock. Her unique beauty and face now held that look that I knew so well. When you witness someone you love dying, part of you is gone too. She couldn't cry. She just stood there, staring into infinity, saying nothing. I hugged her, and Kahina, as if awakened from a trance, hugged me, squeezing me tightly and asking me to stay with her. I felt her shape, her body against mine, her heart beating hard and fast. She was crying and I could feel her little tremors of despair, her breathless breathing, not caring to control her feelings. I was the only trace of normality she could find in an abnormal world, where tragedy is commonplace and peace is extraordinary.

I pulled away from her, gently and carefully, and looked into her slightly swollen eyes. "I have to go to rescue Jlassi. Give me your hands," I said, holding mine out. "I can't go with you and be safe, while Abdar and Olaf risk their lives. I don't want to, once again, watch things happen to people I love. I have to go, do you understand?"

I needed to say it loud and clear, so that I could believe it myself. My soul needed this. I had witnessed my parents die, I had seen Jlassi taken away, and I would not run away while they were going to rescue her. Not this time!

I assured myself that Kahina would be safe with the Tuareg warriors. I did not know this secret path Aleck had mentioned. But she would certainly be safer than me. We would go towards the danger, standing face to face with it, ready to face anything. I could see Abdar's courage. He felt guilty for everything and wanted to help in the solution, whatever the cost. Olaf had an inner strength that aggrandized him and launched him far beyond his stature. He would never let the Tuareg chief down. I think he was always ready to give his life, if necessary. Aleck revealed the

Tuareg fury of dozens of generations. Fear was not part of the Tuareg dictionary, but war was.

Drinking a little from everyone's cup and sipping that strength of the Tuareg spirit, I felt as strong as ever, able to overcome the dread, the crying, the sadness that had plagued me until now. With that borrowed certainty, I said to Kahina, "Go with them and wait for me in Timbuktu. We will be there with Jlassi and I promise I will never leave you again. You know I love you and I don't want to lose you."

"Promise you'll come back to me," she replied. "I love you too, Mádja, and I want you to stay by my side."

Kahina's love at that moment made me even stronger. She gave me a reason to come back, a reason to have courage. That was all I needed to come out of the numbness I was in. I didn't care what happened thinking that life was all tragedy. It gave me a future to fight for with all my strength.

CHAPTER 30

Quietly, Aleck said goodbye to his son, not knowing if he would see him again. He told Abdar to return to the vehicle so they could leave as soon as possible, so as not to lose track of the kidnappers. He stared at the camp, regretting in his heart that he could not properly bury those who died defending the tribe. He felt a deep pain, fearing that he would never see his beloved wife and newborn son again.

* * *

Abdar was driving towards Douentza. We were advancing through North Africa, heading for the last known destination of the bandits. We abandoned the sublime greenery of the banks of the Niger to encounter an increasingly harsh landscape. The sparse trees gave way to houses of golden straw, surrounded by countless baobabs. The ancient giants stood at the side of the road like sentinels, impassively watching our struggle. Along the road, old cars, shattered, crammed with things and people being transported like things. Scraps of trucks in accidents, perhaps with permanent consequences.

No signs, no landmarks—to the right or to the left? We got lost for some time, not knowing where to go. At the moment we needed guidance most, no one was passing by. We talked among ourselves, trying to choose a direction in the middle of nowhere.

In the distance we spotted a vehicle, coming at high speed, and thought it might be the help we so desperately needed. The vehicle came a little closer and Abdar got out of the van, raising his arm to get attention. He began to shout and gesticulate as the vehicle approached, causing the boy to feel his body soften. The jeep passed at almost eighty kilometers per hour on the dirt road. But on board were Kamara and his gang.

"What is it, Abdar? Couldn't you get help?" asked the priest from inside the van.

Abdar, coming out of a trance, answered, "It's them! It's the warehouse bandits!"

In the distance, the jeep turned around and sped back towards us. Kamara had recognized us. Our fate was sealed. But, to everyone's surprise, Olaf pushed Abdar away and, determined, took the wheel.

CHAPTER 31

The priest was fighting a struggle within himself. He had only seconds to decide whether to keep the promise he'd made to his brother or to save people so dear to him. Under the frightened gaze of Mádja and to the surprise of the others, the priest took the wheel. As he drove, he apologized for breaking his promise, in a low voice that could barely be heard, muffled by the roar of the engine of the old car racing down the dirt road. But he made peace with himself and concentrated on the self-imposed task, calling on all his years of training to be able to face that crucial moment.

* * *

The priest knew what to do. He transformed himself as he took the wheel. I could see in his eyes he was getting back to his racing days. He did things with the van that no one else would be able to do. He was cornering at impossible angles, lifting the rear tires off the ground. One centimeter more and the van would have rolled over. It accelerated, tires screeching and kicking up dust before gaining traction and going down the road.

Even though he was wounded, Kamara was holding a submachine gun outside the car. He fired in our direction. He missed most of the shots, but inside the van we could hear the whir of a few bullets bouncing off the body of the vehicle.

The chase continued for a few minutes, and we thought about what to do, because only Aleck had a gun and we knew it wouldn't be enough. By a miracle, and thanks to Olaf's skill at driving, we opened a good distance. In the curves, he made the difference and his trail reduced the visibility of our pursuers. We passed, on the left, near the legendary village of Bandiagara and continued towards cliffs, a couple of kilometers ahead of us.

The priest was in a cold sweat, and every now and then he saw Kamara's jeep looming in the rearview mirror. He kept pushing the van harder than it could handle, until he realized that the engine was starting to fail. Losing the engine there would mean losing his life. He accelerated as hard as he could, pulling the full force of the car. He stopped at the edge of a huge rock where the road continued to the right. He applied the parking brake and spun the tires at high speed, raising a great cloud of dust. He drove off the road and entered a dirt path, between two walls, that took us uphill, until we could not go any farther. From there, we watched Kamara's jeep zooming past below, unaware of the priest's cunning, which had saved us.

The van would not hold. Black smoke started coming out of the engine and our prayers turned to desperation. The extra effort had sealed the vehicle's fate. With no car, no steering, and Aleck nearly dead, there was not much hope. We were surrounded by the legendary Bandiagara cliffs. In front of us, tubular shelters made out of clay filled a giant maw in the cliffs. The priest, a profound connoisseur of Africa, knew where we were. He took a big chance, but in the game of life and death, there are no low stakes.

Aleck had fainted after losing so much blood and his pulse was weak.

Abdar asked the priest what they should do and was desperate, in case the bandits came back. I was scared and thought that this was the end for us. We were left to our own devices. I stared at the mythical figure of Aleck, succumbing to a bandit, greedy for diamonds and revenge. One of my examples of bravery was crumbling right in front of me.

Swallowed by the cliffs, we had nowhere to go. Quiet, we could only hear the ghostly whistling of the wind, channeled by the orange cliffs. Jagged rocks, immense, shaped by the uninterrupted action of nature's blade. The silence of solitude, the chill, and then the inexplicable feeling that we were being watched. The certainty of total dependence on the unknown. Olaf had a spark of hope, because of the memory of a good friend, a researcher and explorer who had lived on those cliffs some years ago. Franz had described in his stories the culture, as well as the geography, of that place in rich detail. Olaf reached for a long stick and went to the middle of the road, where he could be seen. There was no choice. He showed himself in the clearing and said, in French, looking at the cliff, "We are friends of Franz the European. He was with the Dogon until recently. He ate with you, he drank beer with you. The Dogon are made up of those who eat together. Franz told me about the wisdom of Amma. He told me to speak with the pale fox of the desert. We need to talk to Yurugu," concluded the priest, as he drew a square with wavy lines on the ground with a stick.

He used the echo of the cliffs to propagate his message.

One by one, a few men appeared through the gaps in the cliff. Before imperceptible, perfectly camouflaged against the rocks. Some were skillfully climbing down ropes made of baobab fibers. Surrounded, the priest looked at me and Abdar and reassured us that they were peaceful and had come to help us.

CHAPTER 32

John stopped writing for a second and looked surprised at his friend. He shook his head and sipped the last espresso of the day. Staring at the bottom of the cup, as if looking at the past through the coffee grounds, John remembered one time in university, many years ago.

Overhead projector, slide, book, little annotations written down on a piece of paper . . . check! I wonder how many people are coming? he thought, distressed.

The presentation complemented years dedicated to the study of isolated tribes. The Dogon were one of his favorite. He used to love when he encountered new information about them. He then decided that the Dogon would be the object of his first paper at the university. Nothing innovative. It was a literature review of the work of a Dutch explorer who'd lived in the region in the late 1970s.

"Walter E. A. van Beek wrote two books and numerous scientific articles. He experienced daily life on the cliffs of Bandiagara. Today, due to this and other interactions, the

Dogon are used to the foreign presence in their villages. The photos you will see below show the houses, made from a mixture of clay, straw, and goat dung, indistinguishable from cliffs at a distance. Some are accessible only by climbing the cliff, from where they have a privileged view of the horizon. This contributed to the Dogon retaining their autonomy. The first level of small houses is attributed to the Pygmies, who lived on the cliffs more than two thousand years ago, and the larger houses, the most recent ones, were built by the Dogon themselves. My review of the work done by explorers in the region concluded that . . ."

"John? Are you all right?" asked Mádja, interrupting his friend's memories.

"Yes, yes . . . I'm sorry."

Returning from his trance, he looked deep into Mádja's eyes and said, "Life sometimes plays tricks on us that even we doubt. If I told you that the Dogon were the subject of my first big paper at the university, would you believe me?"

"Ah! At this point, my friend, there's no reason to doubt anything," replied Mádja, returning the writer's smile.

"The Dogon are people of peculiar life, with rich and quite complex beliefs. They have ancient knowledge of iron smelting and mathematics and a rich artistic expression through craftsmanship, cave paintings, music, and dance. Really singular people," added John.

* * *

Back at the moment when the Dogon agreed to help us, Aleck was between life and death. In that instant, we needed to trust the priest's intuition and memory.

Upon revealing themselves, the Dogon were not only peaceful as expected, but also offered to help Aleck immediately. Abdar, however, doubted free charity.

"Father? Do you think a fox is going to tell us what we have to do?"

"Of course not," replied Olaf. "But I need them to believe that I believe or at least know that I respect their belief. And be quiet, we need to buy time and also protection. This is not a time for doubt, but for faith."

Aleck, badly wounded and with a very weak pulse, was taken to be treated by the healer. Over a difficult trail, opened by thousands of feet that for centuries had climbed and descended there, a few of the Dogon who had met us carried the Tuareg chief to the sacred place for hunters and healers. An open space on the side of the cliff, where there were, embedded in the wall, several baboon skulls. The animals, once abundant there, no longer existed in the region. I, young and fit, had difficulty keeping up with the pace of the Dogon, who, even carrying Aleck, were faster than me. The priest, short and physically compact, moved along the trails as he had driven the van. He walked in the vacuum of the Dogon, trying to help carry Aleck. Abdar came last, snorting, and the only reason he didn't complain was that he couldn't speak, I think.

Otyuro, the healer, began to macerate an herb and lit the fire, placing a pointed metal object on the embers. His face was painted with geometric designs, mixing white and orange. With a bare torso, the healer was thin from prolonged fasting. He wore a necklace of animal teeth and four feathers equally distanced on his head. He had an air of mystery, of the supernatural, difficult to unravel. He lit seven incense sticks and placed them around Aleck's dying body, then began a ritual murmuring unintelligible words, what I imagined to be ancestral songs.

We watched the ritual next to the priest, who was conversing in French with Lassana, the chief of the tribe. Lassana explained that Franz had left for Europe a little more than six months ago. They were very fond of him and the legacy he'd left: soccer balls for the children and a telescope, which the Dogon used to see into the heavenly realm.

I watched as the mysterious healer stripped Aleck's torso, revealing the wound on his left side, just below the ribs. He reached for the red-hot metal rod and asked us to hold Aleck and put a stick of some kind between his teeth, for him to clench down on at the moment of cauterization. Aleck opened his eyes, semiconscious, dismissed the stick, asked to be released from our grip, and put his hands behind his head, looking firmly at the healer. With a nod, he allowed the healer to proceed. He gritted his teeth, squeezed his eyes shut, and averted his face. The tip of the reddish iron penetrated the wound, cauterizing and cleaning the surroundings with a peculiar sound.

"Ahhhhhh!" groaned Aleck, contracting his abdomen and moving his legs to reduce the pain.

We smelled burning flesh. We watched in disbelief as Aleck handled the situation. Soon after, the healer handed Aleck a calabash, which he said was magical. Inside was a bitter herb tea. The healer then covered the wound with a paste of macerated leaves, which he said would protect him against the evil spirits, called *binu*. Aleck, exhausted, drank all the tea and soon fell asleep, dreaming, perhaps, of his family and the longed-for reunion.

The healer said something in his language, which Lassana translated for us, "Otyuro needs an herb that can only be found in the village of Bandiagara. He says that your friend is possessed, and if he doesn't take this herb by tomorrow, the spirit will take him. I will send two people to the village. And tomorrow morning they will be back here with the plant. Now rest. You will be protected here with us," he said, indicating where we could lie down to sleep. "I will consult the fox and we will talk at dawn."

CHAPTER 33

Late at night, Lassana drew a panel in the sand with several lines, similar to the one the priest had made on the road. At the edge of the drawing, at the end of each line, he placed small sticks that would serve as questions to be answered by the fox. According to the direction in which it walked over the drawing, the chief would get an answer. He left some dried fruit and nuts and went to sleep, waiting for the desert fox.

* * *

The next day we were awakened with the first of the five daily prayers said by the Dogon. I got up and saw, in the dawn light, several men gathered in a structure at the center of the village, which they called the *toguna*, from *togu*, meaning "shelter," and *na*, meaning "big." This was the place where the most important decisions were made. The structure had no walls. It had a very thick, low ceiling, with columns decorated with sculptures of human forms. It was quite peculiar to my eyes. They spoke a language that I didn't know and had heated discussions. At the priest's request, I went to see Aleck, who seemed feverish. He was trembling and sweating profusely. Soon the priest arrived as well, bringing Abdar and the Tuareg who were accompanying us. We stayed at a good distance from the *toguna*, waiting for the meeting to finish. Lassana called the priest and asked him to accompany him during the reading of the answer given by the fox. The priest, respecting Dogon tradition, stayed beside the chief, listening attentively to the interpretation of the signs. Abdar and I looked on, curious, trying to hear the chief's explanation.

"The fox does not lie. It has the knowledge from Amma, and what it says is clear as the new moon. Your friend will face the enemy and survive."

"Good news, then?" replied Olaf.

"Yes and no," answered Lassana. "Leaving the altar, the fox walked straight to his death."

"I understood that it said he would live," reminded Olaf.

"The death it foresaw is not his. It's the death of someone dear to him," Lassana said, in a more serious tone. "It's the death of his heart."

The priest heard the prediction and seemed confused. His engineer's mind, precise and mathematical, told him not to believe any of it. His priest's heart, however, received the oracle with the certainty that it was a true prophecy. He was trying, however, to decipher the exact meaning of the message.

Back in the center of the village, Olaf and Lassana were walking ahead, still talking about the prophecy. Abdar and I, behind, were trying to listen without intruding, when we saw movement on the trail leading to the village. One of the men sent to Bandiagara to get the herbs had returned wounded. Gasping for breath, he stopped and, after recovering, he said, "We were attacked in Bandiagara. We were looking for the herbs for the Tuareg at the market and someone overheard us talking. Minutes later, as we were leaving, we were approached by a man in a red beret. He pointed a gun at us and asked if we'd seen the Tuareg. We denied it, but he didn't believe us."

He paused and, crying, continued, "He shot my cousin in cold blood. He threatened to shoot someone else, randomly, every few minutes, if I didn't reveal what I knew. I was forced to say. Those people were innocent and did not deserve to suffer."

He paused again, trying to contain his emotion to finish the story.

"He told me that he would only leave me alive so that I would bring him the message. He said that the Tuareg chief is to meet him tomorrow at noon in Douentza or he will slit the Tuareg's wife's throat and spread her blood at the entrance to the city for all to see. I'm sorry, I cannot conceive of such evil. He told me that they will wait for the Tuareg chief at the main reservoir in the city. Here is the herb that I hope will save him, otherwise my cousin will have died in vain."

Lassana was devastated. The village had a reputation for being peaceful and they could not remember the last time they had suffered such violence. Yet he vowed to protect the outsiders. He abided by the sacred law of desert lodge and did not blame them for what had happened. He asked the man to give the herb to the healer, who promptly mixed it into a soup of bats and mushrooms and made Aleck drink it all.

Aleck lay down on the stone floor and began to squirm. He groaned and expressed the pain he felt from the effect of the herb. Within minutes, he vomited a greenish-yellow liquid. He was barely breathing. He was sweating too much.

Aleck began to rave, quoting the names of his ancestors and the legendary Tuareg warriors. He said he was crossing the Ténéré, overcoming the dunes of Bilma, dreaming of the oasis of Fachi. He fought against imaginary enemies until he fainted, exhausted, overcome by fatigue.

He fell into a deep sleep, then said disconnected words, grunting in pain, rolling his eyes. The Tuareg chief had hallucinations throughout the day. Beside him, the medicine man was chanting songs that sounded like moans. He enveloped Aleck in the smoke of the mysterious herb.

* * *

In the meantime, Olaf and the Tuareg warriors were discussing how they would meet Kamara. With Aleck wounded and Kamara at an advantage, they could not agree on how they should face him. Abdar and Mádja, with one of the Dogon, went down to one of the nearby villages to look for a vehicle to buy. They returned hours later, celebrating that they had found a car in good working condition. Abdar used one more of the diamonds that he had taken from the Geezer after the fight in the warehouse.

In the late afternoon, sitting on the edge of a row of rocks, they gazed hopelessly at the horizon. The view of the plain was magnificent. The sun was gathering its light mantle, slowly hiding the plain, giving way to the moon, in the eternal dance of the stars. They lay down on the roof of one of the houses. For hours they stared sleeplessly at the stars, awaiting the morning, which was slow in coming.

They witnessed the most beautiful sunrise of their lives, which gradually filled the darkness that reigned over the cliffs with light. The Tuareg were already waiting by the healer's cave. Olaf, accompanied by Mádja and Abdar, came down from the roof and asked about Aleck.

* * *

Everyone looked at the cave entrance and, surprised, we witnessed what, for us, was a true miracle.

CHAPTER 34

While we were waiting for news, Aleck came out of the healer's cave, dressed and ready for the meeting. He looked at us, serious, and, without explaining anything, said, "Let's go get my wife. We have no time to lose. Tonight we seal our fate, and Jlassi will sleep with me again in our tent." He had strength in his voice.

The priest translated his words, and we, perplexed, wondered if all this was really happening. Aleck had gone from certain death to his usual vigor in the space of a day!

The healer, as if he was used to working miracles like that every day, approached us and wrapped each member of the entourage in incense. Protected by the spirits of the bushes, we went down the trail to get the car that Abdar had bought.

A beat-up Toyota Land Cruiser. It could hold five people. The seven of us got in. The priest in the driver's seat, Aleck in the passenger seat, and Abdar, me, and three Tuareg squeezed in the back. At high speed for dirt roads, we drove for more than three hours, until we reached the agreed place.

They were hours of sepulchral silence. Of mixed hatred and fear, of rage and desire for revenge. I admired Aleck and tried to borrow a little of his enormous strength. He, wounded, not knowing if his son was safe, with his wife held hostage by his enemies. He kept his eyes on the road, staring at the horizon, silent, showing neither pain nor suffering.

* * *

Kamara held Jlassi prisoner in an abandoned guard post by the reservoir . She was thrown into a dirty room, with no water, no food, in a half-ruined house that they had taken over without accounting to anyone. They were ready to shoot the first person who asked who they were. This was the place they had intended to bring the Tuareg chief to after their capture. Upon discovering that Jlassi was Aleck's wife, Kamara's obsession increased. He imagined all kinds of horrors he could do to her.

Kamara was also wounded. Without medical help, the cut on his chest began to become infected. He did not feel so strong. He snorted cocaine to keep his energy up and encouraged his soldiers to abuse the Tuareg chief's wife. He used psychological terror, threatening her all the time.

"You will pay for your husband's mistakes," he said, smiling. "My soldiers will show you what a member of the RUF is capable of doing in bed."

Jlassi, frightened, held the necklace against her breast to remind herself of her husband. She thought at every moment of her little son, of the lost hours of breastfeeding and whether he was safe. It was impossible for her to understand the reason for this, the anger against Aleck and the hatred that Kamara harbored against them. She clutched the pendant that Aleck had given her at the fair in Mopti. She had no idea what it meant, but it was the last gift her husband had given her. One by one, the soldiers were fighting for their turn to assault her, until one of them saw the symbol, and exclaimed, "Tigoyú! Tigoyú! Don't touch her, she bears the symbol of Tigoyú!"

Tigoyú was a powerful entity that was said to take over men and force them to have sexual relations with other men. After being forcibly possessed, the man became a woman forever. The circles symbolized the change of gender and the infinity sign, that it was a permanent change. The man was trapped in a man's body, even though he had become, in essence, a woman. This was the legend most feared by the child soldiers. From then on, none of them went near Jlassi again. She was saved thanks to superstition.

At noon, Kamara took the prisoner to the meeting place and waited beside the jeep. The pistol was in his right hand, hiding the deep cut on his left shoulder caused by Aleck. He saw, in the distance, the Tuareg approaching and parking far away.

* * *

Aleck got out of the car and ordered none of us to get out. The Tuareg who were with us protested. They said it was crazy to go alone. Aleck didn't listen to them. He repeated the order and started walking towards the bandits. He called for the priest, who was at a distance where he could still hear him. The dry plain, surrounded by gigantic mountains, created a surreal scenery. The surrounding peaks seemed to be there only to follow the outcome of this story. Aleck looked at the priest and asked him to translate his words to

Kamara. The priest needed a moment to find the right words and said, "This is between you and me. Take me and give me my wife in exchange. She is not part of our dispute. Do what you want with me, but release her and we can all move on with our lives."

Jlassi had always been more than a wife; she was his friend and the confidante of his innermost secrets. The arranged marriage between the tribes could not have been more perfect. Two kindred souls. He represented the tradition and eternal truth of the Tuareg warrior, while she represented the beauty of the nomadic woman, the bridge between the ancient and the modern. Jlassi had studied, she knew another side of life, but she'd chosen the Tuareg tradition when she married Aleck.

"Throw your weapons on the ground, including daggers and swords and whatever you're carrying concealed. Take off your stupid turban and walk towards me," Kamara ordered. "If you do this now, your wife will live."

From what the priest had told me, Aleck never took off his turban in front of anyone. At least, not since he'd started wearing it when he came of age, as was the tradition of his people. The turban, they believed, protected him from the evil spirit that could enter through the mouth. Besides the mystical-religious feeling, the veil indicated social status. Taking off your turban in front of a person, if he was your enemy, was a shameful and extremely humiliating act.

Aleck slowly untied the veil, letting it fall. The wind tried to blow it away, along with his pomp as a warrior and his position as a chief. Without the traditional garment, he looked less like a Tuareg, less like a man. Kamara smiled from afar, rejoicing at the scene. He approached with Jlassi in his arms and motioned for Aleck to come closer to him, to look at him closely for the last time.

CHAPTER 35

Kamara saw this as a chance to complete his revenge. He brought Jlassi close and whispered in her ear, "Your husband is an idiot! I'll kill you first so that he can watch, and then I'll torture and kill him too, to set an example." He turned to the Tuareg. "Nobody defies the RUF and comes out alive!"

"Are you hurt, my love? Did they hurt you?" Aleck asked his wife.

"No! Your gift saved me!" replied Jlassi, looking at the amulet on her chest.

"Allah has guided me!" said Aleck, coming a little closer and opening his arms in the shape of a cross, giving himself completely.

"Stop right there!" said Kamara, pointing the gun at the Tuareg chief. "No surprises this time, or I'll blow your dear wife's brains out."

Jlassi shook her head, disapproving of her husband's decision to turn himself in. Taking aim at the Tuareg,

Kamara entertained the idea of killing both the Tuareg and his wife with one shot.

Jlassi realized that the situation would be final. She looked at her husband, naked, humiliated, ashamed. The man who represented the Tuareg tradition, the warrior, the greatness of his people. The one chosen to lead. With her lips, she spelled "I love you" silently and took advantage of a second of Kamara's distraction to bring her delicate arm behind her, reaching for the pin of one of the grenades he carried in his belt.

She passed her finger through the ring of the pin, as if she were putting on a wedding ring. She prepared her soul for her final act of love.

Kamara looked at the Tuareg chief, and said in a jocular tone, "Last words?"

Kamara pushed Jlassi towards Aleck, planning to shoot the woman in the back, forcing Aleck to look at his wife's face as she was shot. That's when he felt a slight tugging on his chest, along with the characteristic click of a grenade being triggered. He looked at his chest full of grenades and projectiles, in a mixture of despair and surprise. He then let go of his gun, trying to remove his belt. Jlassi tried to run towards Aleck, who, confused, did not understand at the time what was happening. After a long second, a thunderous crash broke the silence, shifting the air in all directions.

The grenade set off by Jlassi exploded, igniting all the grenades and projectiles and turning Kamara into a cloud of smoke, fire, and blood. Jlassi was thrown a few meters in the direction of her husband. As she fell, she received most of the shrapnel, which hit her back and pierced her lungs.

Aleck was stunned, but he was conscious. He saw that his wife's actions had saved his life. The soldiers, frightened by the explosion and the death of their leader, fled. They disappeared, aimlessly, in the dust of the road.

Jlassi, mortally wounded, looked at Aleck and said, gasping, "My love, take care of our son. He will be great in the Tuareg nation. Marry again, give him a mother. Join Kahina. Your lineage will keep our tribes together. Know that I have loved you with all my strength . . ."

"No, Jlassi, no! Stay with me, you can't die. No, no, no, no!" cried Aleck with all the force of his lungs, ignoring his barely healed wound.

He cried, shameless, though a warrior, and screamed to the heavens, asking Allah for an explanation. He took his wife's lifeless body in his lap and stroked her hair. He looked at her delicate and strong face and felt the tragedy of having lost her like that.

Jlassi would have her name sung in Tuareg legends by the fires in the desert. Her tragedy would be transformed into poetry. Verses that would lull the travelers of the desert. And her memory would not be preserved in vain. She would be elevated to the category of ancestral martyrs and warriors. She would sit beside Tin Hinan, the mother of the Tuareg people. She highlighted, with her life and final act, the immeasurable value of women in Tuareg society.

EPILOGUE

"John, I have a surprise for you," said Mádja, looking mysterious.

"I can't wait to find out what it is," John replied, as he sat down at a table on the sidewalk in front of his favorite café.

"Abdar, my brother. You can come," said Mádja to someone inside. "Sit here with us."

"I can't believe it! Abdar, *the* Abdar?" replied John, surprised.

Abdar had been passing through Paris and, as usual, stayed at Mádja's house. He lived in London, but had business dealings all over the world. He visited Paris frequently. He worked in the development of a program of distance education, dreaming to bring quality educational material to the most remote regions of Africa. "It is a bigger-than-life challenge," he said, proudly. "One worth living for." He'd used his famous diamonds to find and bring his family to London, where they were granted political asylum. Abdar gradually built up an online structure. He worked day and night, looking for partners and spreading the dream of seeing

Africa better educated. He believed that only education could save people.

"Yes, that's me! I can't imagine what Mádja has been saying about me," he replied, smiling.

"Of course only good things. Some, however, very serious. You have had a hard time, haven't you?"

"It's true. Now the storm has passed and all this is 'dust in the wind,' as a famous song says," Abdar replied.

"Abdar will help me remember the trip back to Assekrem. And then, how we got to Europe. In four hours, I have to be at the airport. I am going on vacation! After so many years, now I will know what that means. I am going to Iceland to spend two weeks there. Then the Caribbean, because no one is made of stone. Ha! Ha! Ha!" said Mádja, excited. "Nothing like the beach and warmth after a long winter."

"So true, my friend. Come on, the way back to Assekrem. Complicated trip," said Abdar.

* * *

"After the death of Jlassi, we got together and gathered everything that belonged to us. Everything, which was almost nothing. Mádja here, my brother, was as scared as a baby bird fallen from a tree," Abdar said, touching his friend's shoulder. "It was not for nothing. Everything he had been through and yet another tragedy was too much for a teenager's head. He'd started in the caravan as a boy; he ended, however, as a man. On this return to Assekrem, his appearance had changed, his face had another expression, that change that occurs when one understands that the world is infinitely more complex than one imagines. I think, and I have told him this several times, that he decided to overcome all this. Of course, he had to live with the aftereffects of what had happened and he deals with them to this day. But he could have succumbed. No one would say that he had no reason to do this, because he had plenty of reasons to lead a life of self-pity.

"As for Aleck, I was unaware that a man who speaks almost nothing could be even more silent. He was a deeply wounded soul. His movements became slower, the expression on his face empty, as if he were lost. His eyes were heavy, as if he wanted to avoid closing them for fear of evoking the most terrible memories. He was the ghost of the warrior who'd aroused such fear and admiration in us. Alone, and contradicting the tradition in which women prepared the ceremonies, Aleck wrapped Jlassi's body according to the ritual of his tribe and, ignoring the urgency of traveling, decided to bury her with all the honors of a warrior killed in battle. She would rest in the sacred ground of Timbuktu.

"When we arrived in that town, we met up again with the group of Tuareg who had come by the secret road from Niger, among them Kahina," Abdar said, looking at Mádja. "They were waiting for us at the house of Mohamed, brother of the Tuareg chief. At the sad news, everyone paid homage to Jlassi and promised to retell her story in all the caravans from then on. It was a deeply moving moment for everyone. Jlassi was elevated to the category of a legend, a Tuareg heroine. Certainly, she became a song, to be sung during the journeys and celebrations, around the campfires, to the sound of the *imzad*. Moments that Mádja and I remember with great fondness. They said that Aleck should be proud that he had such an honorable and brave wife, which of course did not lessen his pain one bit.

"The funeral was held according to tradition, not before Aleck also paid quick homage to his ancestors, who slept an eternal sleep there. At his wife's grave, he paid his last respects, saying goodbye with these words: 'Go in peace, my beloved. Wait for me. I will be with you when it is my time. For now, I will raise our son as you have asked me to. He will be great among the Tuareg.' He placed on the tomb a carved heart, split in two equal halves. It had been made by Jlassi at the beginning of the trip and represented the union of the two tribes.

"Mádja took advantage of that moment to look for Kahina. She also wanted to see him. They found each other, not bothering to hide their feelings for each other. They hugged and cried together for some time. They needed, however, to pull themselves together and continue their journey. The way to Assekrem would be difficult. Two days at best by car."

* * *

Olaf and Abdar helped with the preparations for the trip and spoke little. The priest thought about comforting Aleck, who always listened to him. But at that moment he felt that the Tuareg chief needed silence more than words.

Mohamed, Aleck's brother, provided two large cars for the trip. Abdar and Mádja made a pact to stay together, to go to Europe as soon as they arrived safely in Assekrem. The priest would continue his mission. He understood that this time of loss and grief would demand more of him, and he was ready to face this further challenge. For two days they faced perhaps the worst stretch of travel in their lives. Silence dominated. The atmosphere was always heavy and serious. The stops were almost automatic: eating, going to the bathroom, and returning to the car.

The arrival at Assekrem was pure desolation. They didn't have the money for the goods, nor did they have the camels, which were extremely valuable. Caravans exist for one reason only: subsistence. The return should have been full of joy for the new goods, the new partners, the gifts collected on the journey, and the reunions that renewed relationships. None of this existed. After months on the road, they'd come back much worse off than when they'd left. Despite the financial tragedy, there was another worse one. The lives lost on the journey, including Jlassi. A nation torn apart by the pain that ravaged them in every way.

Mádja, Abdar, and the priest agreed to meet every week, to catch up, to encourage each other, and to help them get back on their feet. Abdar was still planning to go to Europe, although Mádja secretly wanted to delay his plans to play soccer in order to have more time to spend with Kahina. He had managed to remain in service to her family and maintained daily contact with her. Kahina would now live with the family of an estranged cousin. Every time it was possible, the two would look at each other and think about how they could stay together, overcoming the traditional barriers. With their young dreamers' minds, they made ambitious plans.

A few weeks passed and Aleck decided to retire to Mount Tahat, the highest point in Algeria. He went alone and took very little with him. He found a place in front of the valley from where he could see part of his village. He prayed without stopping, asking for enlightenment: "Allah, the weight I carry is enormous. I believe, however, that you will provide me with the necessary strength so that I do not succumb. A nation depends on me, and so does the universe on you. Give me your wisdom, breathe your strength into me. For me, I give up. For my people, for my son, for you, I am invincible."

On the third day, Aleck returned to camp. It was a dry day and not so hot. He called a meeting of the whole tribe. He invited the elders and announced that he would take Kahina as his wife, if she accepted. Kahina represented the link between the largest Tuareg tribes. She could not refuse. In fact, her refusal would mean more than expressing her will. Saying no to Aleck would represent an embarrassment to all the ancestors and an affront to the decades-long relationship between the tribes. Suddenly she felt mature and embraced her destiny. She agreed to perform the marriage ceremony with the chief of all the tribes. She would guide the son of the legendary Jlassi.

Every choice, however, carries within it an alternative. In deciding for the chief, she rejected the youthful love of Mádja. Kahina thought about the boy one last time and smiled, perhaps realizing how absurd this union would have been. At sixteen, she was gaining the respect of the tribes, finally showing maturity and understanding of the traditions.

The ceremony rekindled a flame that had been extinguished by recent events. The preparations for the feast consumed the tribe's day-to-day life and gradually life returned to a more normal path.

Mádja suffered, but with Abdar's support and constant talks with the priest, he resigned himself. He understood that love could take many forms and that the feeling he had for Kahina should turn into admiration, affection, and a desire for her to be great, as the Tuareg nation deserved to be.

Abdar finally got ready to go to Europe, more precisely to England. He was looking to include Mádja, when a soccer school announced that it would be testing in Tamanrasset, close to where they were.

The priest, who knew Mádja's passion for soccer, remembered one of the boy's requests, which he'd expressed to him in one of the first conversations they had in the caravan. The French soccer school operated in conjunction with a branch of the Christian mission that had been active on the farm where Mádja had lived. Olaf offered to take him to the school if he wanted. Mádja had long dreamed of becoming a player and accepted without blinking.

Mádja took the tests and passed, the only one selected in the screening. With a trip to Paris scheduled, he said goodbye to the priest and to Abdar, promising to see them again one day. He wrote a letter to Kahina, for he knew that with a wedding planned it would be too risky to look for her. From afar, he looked at Kahina with affection, as if taking a picture, and knew that he had registered a precious moment. He set off once again on the road.

* * *

"The rest of the story you already know, John. After I came to France to play soccer and got injured, I was left to my own. I scraped by on the streets and worked in restaurants, until I got the TV job. After I left the TV show, I started working as a tour guide for the hotels and here we are," Mádja recalled.

"Yes, my friend. Here we are! I can't thank you enough for your time and friendship. And you too, Abdar. For doing what you do and being who you are. You could have done whatever you wanted with the diamonds, no one would have said anything. But you decided to give them back in the form of an education. What a great example! Thank you both. Have a good trip to Iceland, Mádja. If you need any tips, let me know, I love that country!" said John, giving them each a big hug.

In that unlikely meeting, three spectacular stories were shared over a coffee table. Unknown by the crowd visiting Paris every day. How many lives are hidden in the universe? How many stories are waiting to be told? John reflected on all this for a second.

A typical Parisian spring morning. A perfect day. One day we will do something for the last time, not knowing that it will be the last. Maybe it won't even be that different. Maybe it won't be charged with emotion and affection. It could just be enjoyed in retrospect. Hugging someone you love for the last time, the last time a son lets his father carry him on his shoulders. The last soccer match with your best friends, or that last family barbecue before you leave home to take over the world.

John watched Mádja and Abdar walk away and smiled. He got up, paid the coffee bill, and said goodbye to his routine of the past month. He walked back to the hotel and prepared his bags for departure. He sat down in the huge hall and remembered the day when Mádja had arrived to start the project. Everything had gone by so fast, in the breath of time that erases days, months, and years. He heard his name called and went to meet the cab waiting at the door.

He said goodbye to Paris, as if it was the last time.

ABOUT THE AUTHOR

Luciano Gouvea was born in the countryside of Minas Gerais on October 18, 1980. After considering a career in soccer, he ended up studying physiotherapy and graduated in 2003. In what would be his last soccer match, Luciano fractured both bones in his right leg and was told that he would have to stay at home for three months without being able to put his foot on the ground! From this accident came his first novel, O Sopro da Crença (The Breath of Belief). The book is a great metaphor of the moment he was living and also of his search for spirituality, very much alive at that moment. Years went by and his second novel languished half-finished. With two daughters and his work and life stabilized, Coração Tuaregue, his second novel, was born. In 2021, dedicating himself more to writing, Luciano also released a book of short stories based on his grandfather, Histórias de um Zé, and is preparing a book of poems and illustrated thoughts that will come out at the end of 2020. A third novel is already in progress and will be based on an incredible true story, and everything indicates that it will be released in the middle of next year. Keep an eye on his Instagram profile, @gouvea_luciano, and also on his YouTube and Spotify channels.

Printed in Great Britain
by Amazon

41240130R00116